THE DEPTH OF THE WATER

The Redemption of Howard Marsh 2

Bob McGough

Bearded Bard Inkworks

www.beardedbardinkworks.com

This arc of the Jubal County Saga could be called
Found Hope.
So each part is dedicated to a different group who helped
me find my Hope as an author.

To my Mothers.
I promise I haven't done all the drugs I write about.
Really. No, really. Y'all raised me right,
despite all my shenanigans.

Contents

An Introduction to Howard Marsh

Howard Marsh is a lot of things: a liar, a thief, a poor man's wizard. He's a shoddily tattooed skin stretched over a too skinny body that's barely held together by the same drugs that are tearing his life apart. A cynic, his words are often as poison as the substances he takes to pass his days, a suicide attempt years in the making.

He's the scion of a family with a history as rich as it is materially poor. He's the product of a miserable county with more dirt roads than paved, where poverty and loss is the order of the day. He's a man haunted by his past, and has yet to find any reason to try and piece himself back together.

You would be well advised to take what he says with a large grain of salt. He will cover the worst parts, glossing over the bits that show his darkest sides. The bits where the drugs that ravage him are in control. Where we find him is at the bottom, eking out a living as a water witch, a copper thief, a finder of lost things. Living in a storage shed and trying to maintain what's left of his frayed relationships with the few family members who will still talk to him.

But dear readers, he's a better man than he thinks. He doesn't see it; he's long forgotten the possibility even, and no one left in his life sees it either. But, if you can endure the miserable existence of watching someone make nothing but bad choices for a time, then you will perhaps be rewarded. Maybe you will see him slowly scrabble out of the muddy, trash filled ditch that is his life.

It won't be quick, and it won't be painless. The stories to come are often filled with sadness. The fairytale ending is not for stories such as these. There is a chance at happiness, but it is a long way away, and there are many obstacles both in him, and in his path.

This is not a plea for understanding, or forgiveness, or any sort of justification. It is just the way of things.

He is Howard Marsh, the Methgician.

And he doesn't give a damn what you think.

THE DEPTH OF THE WATER

Being the Third Tale in the Redemption of Howard Marsh.

Off to a Good Start

Five Months Earlier – April

As my face slammed onto the hood of the car, my vision went black. Just for a split second, but when it came back it was flecked with stars. I didn't notice that as much as I should have, though, thanks to the pain from my tooth, which had just chipped on the cop's side mirror. What I did see was that the specks of light dancing in my vision were a good match for the little splatter of blood that came from my busted lip.

I would have been more pissed but, to be fair, I was giving my best effort at not making it easy for them to load me into the back of the squad car.

Oh, the games we play.

"Goddamn it, Marsh, why do you do this shit?"

Sheriff Snow clearly was not well pleased. He ran a hand through the thinning remains of his graying hair. That was the only part of him that could be described as "thin," that was for damn sure. His gut was truly a wonder, straining the buttons of his uniform to almost lethal levels. I was half afraid that at any moment one might pop off with enough force to take my eye out, which, considering the pain in my mouth at that moment, might have been a blessing.

I shifted in my chair. The questioning room at the sheriff's department was not known for its comfortable choice of seating. And when you're handcuffed it is not easy to improve that situation, no matter how much you squirm.

Gingerly running my tongue over my chipped tooth, I realized I was still feeling contrarian. It was as if what little fuck I had left to give had been living in that now missing part of my tooth. "You know, there's got to be a good fifty Marshes in the county. How come I'm the one everyone just calls 'Marsh'?"

Snow heaved his bulk into the chair across from me, the wooden chair creaking ominously. " 'Cause in a long line of weirdos and fuckups, you take the cake." He tapped a fat fingertip down next to the Styrofoam cup of coffee that was the table's only decoration. "This being a case in point. All we wanted was for you to come answer some questions, and now I have you on assaulting an officer."

"Y'all gonna pay to fix this tooth?" I asked, leaning forward and parting my lips as wide as they would go. I knew the sight had to be something awful. I doubted he could even tell which of my few remaining teeth was the one that had been chipped—if he could see them at all past the swollen lip.

Snow's mouth curled in disgust as he glared across the battered table. "How about this: You answer my questions, you do a good job, and we forget about the assault charge. Jim's eye will be black a day or two, but he said he'd give it up just to have you out of here. As for the tooth, you can forget about that. Call it a stupid tax."

If I could be said to have a nemesis, it would be Sheriff Snow, though I doubt he would view it the same way. It's like when I was in school, our archrival in football beat us something like thirty years in a row. We hated them. Well, the school did—I couldn't much be troubled either way.

They beat us *thirty years* in a row. They were our most hated foe. But to them, we were nothing—just a slight bump in the road. They had all the cards, and you can't work up a hate against someone you beat up all the time.

Snow made my life hell. But in truth, he always had the winning hand. So whereas he was the thorn in my side at all times, I was just one of the dozens of screwball druggies this county had to offer. And the odds were always in his favor.

"Fine," I relented. No point in fighting the inevitable, no matter how riled up I was feeling. Especially if it would help me avoid a bit of jail time.

Snow nodded, though the sour look never left his face. He snapped his fingers and the deputy that had been standing in the corner of the room came and set a yellow legal pad and pen on the table in front of him. Luckily the table was bolted to the floor, so when the man leaned forward his gut didn't slide it into me.

Taking the pen in hand, he readied himself to take notes. "So, Marsh, let's talk about Angie Burdette."

I could feel my eyes go wide. "Shiiiit."

TREAT YOURSELF

Six Months Earlier – March

It took me some time to realize that all I had done for the past hour was mindlessly doodle on my dry erase board. I was working on sigils, I guess, though I was erasing them as soon as I did them. If I looked hard enough I could see the faint outline of a few of them where I had done a shit job wiping them away, but for the most part the board was just as smudged as my hands. Regardless, they all looked like shit.

HD said practice would make perfect, but I was already over it, and this is the first time I'd tried my hand at it in weeks.

It had been a good five days since I had slept for more than a few moments at a time, and in truth I was showing no signs of really slowing down. My mind was racing but in strange, circular ways, and I wasn't really enjoying myself anymore. I had reached the point of the high where I really just wanted to sleep for about twelve hours. The meth was coursing too strong in me to allow anything like that, though, unless I could find some way to burn off the excess energy it was giving me.

You ever been too high? Or too drunk? And then you hit that moment where you would give just about anything to be sober, so you end up going slam to pieces right in the middle of the party? So then your cousin, who drove you there, is trying to talk you down, but instead you just puke on the carpet of Jane Kelley's new trailer? And when she starts shouting at you for messing up her housewarming party, you end up throwing up on her, too?

Just me?

Well, I wasn't there yet, but I was close.

It was one of the rare days that it actually felt nice inside my storage unit home. About one week in spring and one week in late fall were the only times, it seemed, that weren't too hot or too cold in here, so I had decided to make the most of it by staying up through the whole time of it. But now I'd had my fill, and more, so it was time to give it a rest.

A flicker of an idea came to me, and I grinned. I wasn't sure what time it was, but glancing out the roll-up door I could tell it must have been midmorning, maybe lunchtime at the latest. I stepped over and peered out. My "neighbor" Corey Davis's car was gone, and it looked to me that I was alone there in the U-Store-It.

Stepping back in, I went over to the footlocker I kept in the back by the little minifridge. It was buried under a pile of "treasure," of course—mostly books and a few bits of flotsam and jetsam liberated from the Christian Mission drop-off. I had to dig it free, the lock on it rattling as I pulled it from the pile. With a twiddle of my fingers, the lock on it pulsed with a faint purple light and then popped off, clattering onto the concrete floor. Reaching in, I pulled out a handful of old porno mags, the last of what remained of what had been a rather impressive collection back when I was in high school.

Folks always talked about internet porn, but I was a traditionalist at heart.

I also didn't have internet. Crazy how the cable company will refuse to provide service in a storage shed for a guy who'd never made an on-time payment in his life. Some folks just hate to make money, I guess.

Resuming my spot in my broken recliner, I began flipping through until I found who I was looking for: Katlyn Fox, the big spread in the March '99 issue of *Hound Magazine*. Folding out the centerfold, I eyed it over one good time, trying to memorize every detail.

Once I had, I shucked my pants and closed my eyes. I set about breathing as slow as my meth-addled body would let me, keeping as still as I could. Under my breath I voiced a few low words and concentrated on the mental image of Katlyn Fox. I just kept repeating those words, picturing her naked body as I felt a trickle of drug-fueled energy start to flow from my fingertips.

I opened my eyes then. Instead of a grungy storage room, I was in a solid white room. And instead of being alone, Katlyn Fox was standing there, giving me a private nude dance.

It was going to be perfect. The illusion would drain the last of the excess energy, and if I timed it just right I would get off and then go to sleep. And if Katlyn's dancing was almost a move-for-move copy of one my ex, Lidda, had given me while we were still together, well, a good illusion is always based on fact.

Grinning wide, I took things in hand and got down to business. There is a special sort of buzz that comes along with using magic that accents that hyperactive meth high. I could feel my body converting all that extra juice into something primal, something eldritch, and it felt . . . well, if not good, at least not bad.

Katlyn was saying my name now, leaning in close.

This illusion was supposed to be silent, but drugs have their own way of adding little sparks of life.

"Howard Marsh? Mr. Marsh?" she yelled questioningly.

That was weird. She didn't sound anything like I would have thought. It was getting pretty disconcerting, to be honest.

"Oh my God! I'm so sorry!" she said, her voice filled with horror.

Then it hit me. Someone had walked up.

Shit.

With a breath, I dispelled the illusion and lunged for my pants. With the spell gone I could see there was a young woman standing at the entrance to my shed, her back turned to me. Her hands were thrown up like blinders, and she was profusely apologizing over and over.

I didn't respond until I had my pants back on, which was a thankfully brief amount of time. Covered back up, I faced her back. "You can stop apologizing. If I'd had any sense, I'd have closed the door. Just was real nice out, is all," I said sheepishly.

She slowly turned, lowering her hands, and I started to freak out. I could see that she was pretty young, maybe not even eighteen. Had I just exposed myself to a teenager? They were gonna bury me under the fucking jail this time.

"Please, God, tell me you're eighteen," I said.

She looked confused a second, then repulsed. "Are you hitting on—?"

"*Fuck* no!" I shouted, cutting her off. "It's just . . . what you just saw . . . if you aren't . . ."

Realization dawned on her face. At least I'm pretty sure it did. It was hard to tell with all the makeup she had on. She looked to be going through some sort of goth phase, which I'll admit I had briefly toyed with in my high school career, so no judgement there. I guess.

"I'm eighteen," she said tartly. She was a tiny little thing but made up for it with all manner of loud accessories and makeup. A Marilyn Manson shirt coupled with some sort of chain-covered pants that probably came from the Hot Topic in Montgomery completed the look. She was such a cliché and she had no clue. It was delicious.

But then I was the guy beatin' off in the storage unit he lived in, so maybe I should climb down off my high horse a bit.

She bent over and picked up a notebook that she must have dropped in her rush to cover her eyes. "So, yeah. I'm sorry. Again."

I sighed, pulling a mostly empty pack of smokes from my pocket. "Well, since I have managed to make an impeccable first impression and I assume you have a real good reason to come here, maybe let's skip all the pleasantries."

She stepped fully into the shed. "I'm Angie Burdette."

Mating cigarette to lighter, I took a first blessed drag of smoke into my lungs. "How are you kin to Thomas Burdette?" Tom was sorta a friend of mine, I was pretty sure. I hadn't seen him in a while, and that often boded that I had done something I ought not to have in one of my benders. The same age, we had been in school together and kept up with each other whenever we crossed paths.

"He's my oldest brother," she replied.

"Shiiit, I didn't even know he had a sister." I reached out my hand to shake hers. She eyed it with undisguised horror, and I remembered what I had been doing with that hand when she had walked up. I lowered it quickly.

"Half-sister, actually. I lived with my mom until a couple of years ago." She was clearly regaining her footing a bit as her tone changed to something between annoyed and fully sour. I fancy myself a pretty fair judge of character, and my quick read on her was she was a bit of a negative Nancy.

Regardless, that explained why I wouldn't remember her. "Alright. So why are you here?"

Let Sleeping Dogs Lie

Today – September

The sound of a car pulling up, its tires crunching noisily over the gravel of the U-Store-It lot, is what woke me up. Knowing that no one ever visited except HD, and having not gotten a call from him saying he was on the way, I decided to go back to sleep. More likely than not it was someone popping into my neighbor's bootleg accountant shop, so I just continued to try and doze in my recliner.

Two car doors shutting later, I could feel someone staring at me.

"I know you're awake, boy, show your company your manners." I knew the voice instantly, which gave me a powerful incentive to do the exact opposite out of spite. The voice belonged to Mike, far and away the least favorite of my uncles.

Cracking an eye open, I saw him standing there in the entryway with a short, round little man I did not recognize. "Manners? Fuck are those?" I was feeling a bit snarky, having been woken up from a rather pleasant nap.

Mike rolled his eyes and walked on in. "Howie, this is Frank Burdette." He fucking knew there were few things I hated more than being called "Howie."

Peering closer, I realized I did know the man, but that was several years and likely sixty plus pounds ago. The years had not been kind to Frank. "Mr. Burdette. Been awhile," I said, sitting up straight.

Mike sat on the cot and motioned for Frank to join him. The man did so hesitantly, speaking as he sat, "It has been. Since around you and Thomas's graduation, I guess."

My uncle Mike was the relative I got along with about the least, and that was really saying something. We'd pretty well hated each other for as long as I could remember, so we avoided each other as much as possible. He was a churchgoer—one of the only ones in the family, really—and you always had the feeling he thought he was better than the rest of us. It rankled me, to be honest.

"That'd be right. So what brings y'all out this way?" We could have drawn out the pleasantries, but I had it in mind to get back to my nap as quickly as possible rather than hang out with Mike.

"I, uh, well—" started Frank.

Mike cut in, "Mr. Burdette wants to hire you to find his daughter. It's been six months and the cops have gotten jack squat done about it."

"I know you saw her not long before she . . ." The man swallowed painfully. You could tell it was really eating him up. "And I've heard you have a knack for finding things. There is a reward out that our job"—he gestured toward Mike—"has put up. Fourteen thousand dollars. If you find her, that's yours. As would be another four or five thousand I could scrape up, I think. And, if it's needed, I can give you five hundred right now as an advance."

Mike waved a hand, cutting him off again. Typical Mike. "He will give you three hundred up front. And if you don't find her, you best had pay every cent of it back, boy. And if I find out so much as a nickel has gone to drugs, then I'll whip you up and down this county."

I looked pointedly at Mike, then leaned back in my recliner and closed my eyes. The mock snoring might have been excessive, but I feel it helped get my point across. I swear I could hear the steam coming outta Mike's ears. The man knew better than to argue with me, so I wasn't surprised when I heard him huff and storm out of the shed.

When I didn't hear Frank follow, I cracked one eye. The man was still sitting on the cot, pulling a handful of bills from his wallet that he set on the bed in a neat pile.

I laid off the act as he rose to his feet. My eyes were on that money, which I could certainly have used, but my damn conscious decided to make one of its rare appearances. "I find things, not people, Mr. Burdette. I can't take your money."

He looked at me. "I heard the cops were a little rough on you. Thought that might help get your tooth fixed."

I sat up. I glanced out at the car where my uncle was sitting impatiently. "Mike tell you that?"

He nodded hesitantly, his chins jiggling as he did so.

I slid my tongue over the tooth, which was a righteous bitch every time I ate or drank anything hot or cold. A fixed tooth would have been nice, but so far drugs had been nicer. Impulsively, and definitely against my better judgement, I rose to my feet.

"I reckon it won't hurt to try." I extended my hand, which he took in his sweaty grasp. "I make no promises, though. And that money there—I ain't payin' it back one way or the other."

"That's fine, that's just fine!" He pumped my hand up and down. "Thank you!"

He seemed on the verge of tears, so I extracted my hand as quickly as I could. "Mike is waiting for you," I said with a nod toward the car where my uncle was glowering at me.

Frank handed me a business card. "Here is my number. Call anytime, anytime at all."

The car horn honked. I flipped Mike off.

"Thank you again," said Frank as he waddled to the car.

"Sure thing," I responded. I looked down at the card and, suddenly angry at myself, flicked it onto the bed. As soon as their car pulled away, I crawled back into my recliner and resumed my nap.

First Impressions

Six Months Earlier – March

Angie looked me up and down. I could see distaste flickering around the edge of her face, but she made a slight effort to conceal it. "Thomas said you would be a good person to talk to."

"Huh." I guess he wasn't mad at me after all. Or maybe, based on my impression of the girl, he *was* and this was my punishment. "First time I can recall someone saying that. I ain't much for small talk with strangers."

"I'm not here for small talk," she said, losing a small, exasperated sigh. "I want to talk about Cernunnos." The way she said it, it came out like "Cern-u-nos."

I was caught a fair bit off guard by that. "What?"

"Cernunnos, you know, the Horned God?" For a girl who had come to me, it was amazing how snarky and acrid her voice was becoming. She had clearly written me off as a loss but had come too far to go back empty handed now.

"Yeah, I do, though I don't say it that way. What about him?" I was very, very leery of where this was going.

"Well I'm pagan, and he's my patron god, you know, so I have some art of him up on my wall. Thomas saw it and said he had seen stuff like that before. I was surprised a redneck like him had ever seen anything like that before, but he said you would be someone to talk to about it."

"You have art . . . of him? On your wall?" My stomach began to churn.

"Of course!" she snapped. She opened up her notebook and started flipping through it. "Gives me something to focus on when I pray to him. I draw him all the time."

She held up her notebook and splayed it open, showing me where she had drawn a horned . . . *something* going through the woods. She was clearly no artist. I supposed all the relevant parts were there, though—the horns, the bones—but there was no sense of menace. It was almost like he was out for a stroll, off to pick daisies.

"I feel so close to him, and there are no other pagans I know that worship him. I have a few Tumblr friends in the pagan community that do—that's where I found out about him, actually. But around here"—the way she said "here" told me all I needed to know about her views on

Jubal County—"there's nothing. There's only two other pagans even at my school. Back in Birmingham there were tons. Here . . . ugh."

I was still confused. "So you came here why?"

She rolled her eyes at my denseness. "I told you, I am looking for others like me—folks that worship Cernunnos. I thought you might be one, 'cause of what Thomas said."

"You worship him? Why?" My confusion was not lessened.

I swore for a moment her eyes went dreamy. It was . . . . disturbing. It was the moon-eyed look young men and women got over their first love. "I can relate to him in ways most people could never understand. A god of nature and death . . . that's my aesthetic. And when he talks to me—"

I cut her off. "He *talks* to you?"

She frowned at being interrupted. "Well not in words, but in feelings, you know. And little signs that pop up all over the place. Is that not your experience?"

I shook my head. There was so much wrong here I didn't know where to begin. "First off, what's that bit about a god of death? How the hell did you come by that?"

Her eyes narrowed. "Uh, 'cause that's what he is."

"Says who?" I frowned.

"Says everyone I've talked to about him."

I had seen Cernunnos, or rather a tiny sliver of him. Not something you ever, ever wanted to deal with. And while death is a frequent result of such dealings, that was not because he was some death god. That was just the price of doing business with beings so far beyond human that they tended not to even notice when their actions ended one of us, much as we would slap a fly and forget about it seconds later.

"People on Tumblr?"

She huffed. "Yes. But they know their shit. The pagan community on there is—"

I cut her off again. "Probably full of shit. You are fucking with shit you need to stay well clear of. You think Cernunnos gives you little signs, little feelings? Bullshit. Why the fuck would a being so far beyond you give even the tiniest fuck about your petty bullshit?"

She'd made me mad, far madder than I would have thought possible, and I wanted her gone. "I think you got pissed at Mommy and started acting out. She making you go to church, so you decided to go pagan instead? Wanted something to make you different? Kept on till you got sent back to live with Daddy?"

I could tell by the way she flinched that some of that had hit home. She was also getting really pissed. I decided the best answer I could give was to take off my shirt. Ripping it off and throwing it to the ground I leaned close, tilting my shoulder to her. Five ragged scars, each about a half inch wide, scored my shoulder down into my back. "That's the kind of sign the Horned God gives, not some fucking feeling."

The anger bled from her face as she saw the scars. She reached out haltingly for a second as though she wanted to touch them. Instead of fear in her eyes, though, I saw wonder. "How did that happen?" she asked, her voiced dazed.

I straightened up. "I had the bad luck to be around him one day. Bad luck, but the good sense to stay the hell away after that."

She was ignoring my words; instead, her eyes were locked onto my chest where, just above my heart, was a brand. A brand of the Horned God. One that I certainly had not asked for, just as I had not asked for the crow brand on the other side of my chest.

"Are you a priest?" she asked. "Could you take me to him?"

"Get the fuck out of here."

She heard me but was still staring at my chest.

"GET THE FUCK OUT!" I screamed at her.

Her eyes grew large and she stepped back. "What the hell, man?"

My jaw was so tight I could hardly talk. "If you do not get the fuck out of here right goddamn now I will hurt you. I will hurt you very, very badly."

She opened her mouth, but seeing the look on my face she just turned and scuttled away, holding her notebook tightly to her chest.

Three days later, she went missing.

WHAT WE ALL COME TO NEED

Today – September

I woke up from my nap to find it was getting on toward evening. It had grown pretty dark in my shed, the sun having begun to set behind it. I could hear the crackle of a static-ridden TV, so Corey must have made it back and was attempting to get channel twelve again. I thought about joining him but instead decided that now was as good a time as any to start hunting down Angie.

I was positive that if I found her, I would not like where she had gone. The only consolation I had going for me was the knowledge that she had not managed to find Cernunnos. Had she, someone from the family would have gotten word to me. But wherever she had gotten off to, the trail would start down that path.

Grumbling to myself, I got out my phone and spent a few of my precious minutes potentially getting a ride. Liam was a younger guy, barely out of high school, so I could usually bum a ride or two in exchange for buying him beer and smokes. I was in luck—he agreed and would be along after a bit. I decided to explore my little box of oblivion that lived under my recliner and see what sort of mental exploration I could get into while I waited.

By the time Liam's battered Caprice pulled up to my shed, I was humming right along.

As I climbed in, the boy already had a lit cigarette waiting for me. Taking it in hand I took a long drag, letting its menthol coolness wash over me. "You know me so well," I grinned.

Liam nodded, grinning a bit. "Yeah, yeah. First beer and smokes, then I'll take you where you want. Cool?"

"Cool," I agreed.

There was a Marathon a half mile from my storage unit, so within five minutes almost all of a suitcase of Natty Light was safely ensconced between us, the two missing bottles cracked open and tucked between our legs.

It was good and dark now, so dark that it mixed with my cocktail of drugs and beer and the edges of Liam sorta blurred, his dark skin blending in with the darkness of the car's interior. "So, where to?" the young man asked.

"The weird kids still hang out over by the bridge?" I asked. I didn't have to tell him which bridge; Jubal County is not exactly awash with opportunities for the younger set to occupy their time in a wholesome manner. So the place to be if you were around high school age on a Friday night—at least near Elk Grove—was Mary Daniel Bridge.

"Yeah. Why? Missing your people?" he joked.

I laughed. "Maybe I am. Anyways, let's hit the bridge."

"Fine by me. What I had planned anyways," he said as he put the car in drive.

We rode with the windows down, rap coming from the speakers. Kid Cudi, Doomtree, stuff like that. Hip-hop wasn't my favorite, but there were a few artists I just loved to fucking death, and they were two of them. We both sang along to "Pursuit of Happiness," singing the words out the windows so that our shitty voices were quickly lost in the wind.

Ten miles after leaving the outskirts of Elk Grove we turned onto a rutted dirt road. The Caprice's shocks groaned in protest at the rough ride, but Liam hardly slowed. He just finished his beer and tossed the empty out the window.

It was a Friday, and it was also after a home football game, so the bridge should have been fairly jumping. There was an uneasy truce between the folks who frequented it and the cops most times. So long as the people at the bridge didn't cause no trouble and no kid wrapped a car around a tree in a drunken mess, they were left alone. Besides, in a town so in love with football as the Grove, you didn't go harassing your players, not after a big win like Liam had said tonight was.

And hell, most of the cops had hung out at the bridge themselves growing up.

As we neared it, Liam slowed the car. I could see the headlights of a few vehicles, but it was a general rule that for every car you saw headlights for, there would be two or three others parked alongside the road. Not everyone could afford a decent battery.

Liam pulled up behind a dark-blue boxhead Chevy and put the car in park. Scooping up the rest of the remaining beers, he tossed me one. "I'll find you before I leave, see if you need ride back."

Catching the beer, I thanked him and we parted ways.

Segregation lives on in the South in strange places. Like when you finish a Coke and there are just a few drops left, each caught in separate little puddles at the bottom of the bottle. The bridge was one of those places.

Music pulsed through the air, coming from several different cars. At the end of the bridge, where Liam had walked over to, was where the Black kids hung out, the steady thump of speakers rattling one of the trunks. As I walked by, moving from car light to shadow and back again, I nodded to a few that I knew.

Stepping onto the bridge proper, the sounds of rap blended with blaring country as I entered the land of white kids. There wasn't any real animosity between the two groups since these people would all be in class together on Monday or had played football together earlier that night, but when left to their own devices they tended to separate. It was just one of those things you found in the South, least out in the country.

I had done drugs with a lot of these kids' older brothers . . . and fucked a few of their older sisters as well. Which, seeing as how much bigger a lot of them were than me, I was probably lucky they didn't know. Fucking hormones in the chicken, making them big these days. I spotted one girl swaying in the headlights of a jacked-up truck, clearly drunk off her ass. I just shook my head. 'Cause clearly I was one to judge.

Crossing the bridge, I saw a small fire burning in a rusted out barrel off to my left. The creek that the bridge went across was rarely more than five or six feet wide, while the bridge itself was a good forty. There was a good bit of sandy space to either side of the stream, and it was down there that the kind of people I would be looking for might be.

As I eased myself down the embankment, following a well-worn path grooved out by countless booted feet, the familiar, beloved smell of pot reached my nose. I could see a trio of youths standing around the fire, one passing a joint to the girl to his left. A few more folks were lounging around on the edges of the light. I was pretty sure at least one girl was giving a guy a discreet handy, but out of politeness I didn't stare.

Easing my way up to the fire, I positioned myself between the girl currently taking a hit and the guy to her left. All three eyed me pretty warily, likely because I was a good ten years older than them. The girl coughed twice, holding the joint between her fingertips.

I arched my eyes. "Gonna pass it?"

She looked at the guys. One shrugged; the other just stared. Hesitantly she passed it to me, and I set about filling my lungs. It was skunkweed, but any port in a storm, I say. Holding it in, I fought back a few coughs then slowly exhaled, a plume of smoke blending with the smoke of the fire. I then handed it off to the guy next to me and cracked open my beer. Raising it in a mocking sort of toast, I winked and took a sip.

These were the goths, the punks, the metalheads. Probably the entire population of them in northern Jubal County, or if not, damn near it. I was a little surprised there were as many as there were down here, to be honest; in my day it was just me and about three others. There had to be at least ten folks, maybe a few more I couldn't really see.

Oh, how the times, they are a-changing.

"I heard a couple of you were pagans," I said, deciding to not beat around the bush. Why use subtlety and tact when you can simply blunder about?

The girl gave me a funny look while the guy directly across from me snorted. "I think you mean Satanists." He pulled a necklace from inside his shirt and jangled it at me. A tiny gold upside-down cross hung from it.

"Nope. I said pagans. I ain't got time for lightweights." I could have perhaps been a bit more politic, but the guy had already gotten on my nerves.

"Fuck you, dude," he spat back at me. "Fuck do you know about shit?"

"More than you, I can promise you that." I looked around the area—all eyes were on us. I raised my voice. "The Burdette girl told me she had two pagan buddies. I need to find them."

I got back silence by way of response. After a few heart-beats, my Satanist buddy spoke. "You trying to find her?"

I nodded.

"You a cop or something?"

I laughed so hard I thought I felt a little pee trickle out. "First time I ever been accused a' that," I gasped out. Still giggling, I managed to follow that with, "Consider me something like a private detective, and you'll be close enough."

The girl at my side spoke up. "You want Mike and Lily, then."

I gave a little nod her way. "They around?"

She blushed a little. "They, uh, went under the bridge."

They were fucking, then. "Well, looks like y'all get some company, then, till they come out. Lucky y'all." I grinned. They groaned.

And They Say Romance Is Dead

By the time the two slunk out from under the bridge, I had the Satanist kid about ready to fight me. I was so into riling that kid up that I almost didn't notice them ease out from under there as discreetly as they possibly could for two people that everyone already knew had been getting frisky. Luckily, though, I caught a flash of white as the boy, Mike, pulled his shirt back over his head.

" 'Scuse me," I said to the angry little Satanist, cutting him off mid-sentence. Without another word I wheeled and struck out across the sand to the two lovebirds who I could see had spotted me coming toward them. They were standing with a woman, a stupidly tall skinny type who likely had an honest-to-God foot and a half on me. She was a bit younger than me, but clearly a bit older than everyone else here. Probably one of those can't-let-the-glory-days-of-high-school-go types. She was talking to them in a low voice, likely filling them in on the ruckus I had been causing.

They eyed me warily but otherwise held their ground. Striding up, I extended a hand. "Mike? Lily?"

They nodded, and Mike took my hand. "I think I know who you are. You're Gerry's cousin, right? Howard?"

"Yep. He's my first cousin. I'd forgot he was about all y'all's age." Gerry was another one of those very rare members of my family that were of some account. Churchgoer, straight As—you know, one of them annoyingly perfect types. I loved him to death, but for some reason he had never really took to me.

Lily spoke up. "Anna said you were looking for us?"

Anna must have been the tall woman, then. I noticed Lily refused to take my hand. I had a suspicion Angie told her about our meetup that time, which was just hypocritical to my mind, considering why I had just had to wait on them. Or maybe she just was an unfriendly type. Either way, I decided I didn't much like her.

"Yeah. I only met Angie the once, but I know what she was on about. She mentioned y'all, not by name, though. I figured, way she was acting, she like as much didn't have many friends. Figured she prolly clung to you two."

"Well she was still pretty new," offered Mike.

"Son, if she had come here in the third grade, she'd still be considered new. But that ain't neither here nor there. Now I am sure the cops have prolly talked to you a time or two. But I ain't a cop, and all the shit they think is bullshit, well, that's what my wheelhouse is. I've been hired to find her, and that's what I aim to do. So what can you two tell me? That you prolly couldn't tell those tight-ass cops."

They looked at each other. I feel like they was having a whole conversation there in tiny shrugs and little head moves. But then I *was* pretty high.

Mike looked back to me after a moment. "She was trying to find Cernunnos."

Confirming what I already knew. "I figured that as much, and that's prolly partly my fault."

Lily's face was split with a frown. "Yeah, when she came back from seeing you that time, she became all convinced he was running around the woods. Before, she had just been trying to find someone else like her."

The tall girl, Anna, laughed. "There was no one like her."

Lily punched the taller girl's arm. "Shut up!"

"What? I meant that in a good way," Anna said.

Lily glared at her.

"Mostly, anyway. I mean, you gotta admit, she could be a real bitch sometimes." I swear Anna then said, "Most times," under her breath. Her, I liked.

Lily rolled her eyes and started to pointedly ignore the taller girl. "My point is you got her all excited and looking around, then she disappeared. So it's exactly your fault, which is what I told the cops."

I had wondered how they made the connection exactly. Well, now I knew. "Thanks for that, by the way. Still got a broke tooth from it, so good job."

"Well she's still missing, so good job." Point: Lily. Yep, did not like this girl one bit.

I just skipped over that statement. "Where was she looking, then?"

Mike chimed in. "We used to go ghost hunting a lot. Then she got this theory that Cernunnos might be near a haunted house or something. That those were places where the veil was thin. We went with her a couple times, but the day she went missing, we . . . uh . . . had a date."

You ever hear about a house being haunted, it probably isn't. Us humans, we have a defense mechanism. Any place that's actually haunted, or twisted up in something supernatural, we avoid like the plague. It's a subconscious thing. You want to find something spooky? Go down a road no one ever goes down, not one that people tell stories about.

So whatever place she was going to was prolly not where she got into trouble. But it might be someplace near there. Some out-of-town girl was not gonna know the more secret nooks and crannies of Jubal County, just the bigger stories like the Haint and the McGregor House. "She give y'all any idea where she might have wanted to head that day?"

Lily answered, "Look, we already told the cops all this, so you're just wasting your time. And ours. Come on, Mike." She grabbed his arm and started to tug him away.

I was left standing in the looming presence of Anna, sighing as they walked away.

"You don't remember me, do you?" the tall girl asked.

I swear I damn near had to crane my neck up to see her face. But then, I was high enough that my depth perception was a bit wonky. Jeans, black band shirt with an indecipherable logo, leather wrist cuff, and long blonde hair framing a pretty face with sharp green eyes was what confronted me. A face that was oddly familiar.

"Maybe? You seem sorta familiar," I replied.

She smiled. "You dated my sister a bit. I'm Anna Wilkerson, Amy's sister."

"Oh, shit, you are! Man, you done shot up like a sprout!" Thinking back, as Amy and I hadn't seen each other in about five years, that would make Anna about . . . twenty-three. Maybe? And while Amy had been taller than me, too—that whole family was fucking tall—none of them were as tall as Anna. "How is Amy? Still talking of me fondly?"

She laughed, hands in her pockets. "Hell no. When you do come up, it's mostly just cuss words and regrets."

"Sounds about right. And how about you? What're you up to these days, other than tree impersonations?

Anna shrugged. "This and that—you know how it goes. I'm taking classes up in Montgomery now, gonna be a nurse."

"Well I'll be . . ." I had no idea where to take the conversation from there. She was cute in a weird way, but I had other matters on my mind. A lull came between us as I pondered what to say.

Anna broke the silence. "Sorry about Lily. She can be a huge bitch too. I know where Angie went that day, though. Lily talked about it a lot when it first happened."

I perked up noticeably. "Really? And just where was that?"

She grinned, shaking her head. "I'm pretty much over this place, and the night is young. How 'bout I just show you?"

I didn't really want a sidekick, but then the lack of car was, as ever, a hindrance. And who knows? Maybe she'd be as much fun as her sister . . .

"Alright, but you're driving," I said with a laugh.

"Still don't have a car?" she smirked. "Deal."

Howard Marsh, Patron Saint of Partying Weird

We were barreling down Highway 31 in her little blue Ford Focus with some sort of growling black metal roaring up out of the speakers. I was pretty partial to heavy metal myself but preferred it slow, doomy. But this—I couldn't understand a word they were saying, not a one. Anna just seemed to be wild about it, though, and seeing as she was driving and letting me bum smokes, who was I to complain?

She thankfully turned the music down a bit. "You know, my sister, she used to tell all sorts of stories about you."

"Mostly lies, I'm sure. I'm a saint, I promise." I winked at her, but she was watching the road.

She laughed. "Right, Howard Marsh, patron saint of partying weird."

"Gotta be good at something, I guess," I said. It was too dark to look out the side window, which was my preferred method of travel, so I just watched the road, too, keeping an eye out for deer.

"What do you say after I take you by this place, we do some partying?" she asked.

There was an invitation in there, I could feel it. I looked over at her in time to see her looking back to the road from where she had been looking at me. I thought I saw an arched eyebrow. It was pretty dark, though. The physics involved with a girl that tall . . . well, it was too intriguing a prospect to turn down. Even if she was four or five years younger. I suspected there was some sort of game going on here, likely between the sisters. But I didn't much care; Amy and I were not on speaking terms as such.

Cautiously, I nodded. "Alright, sounds good to me. We got much farther to go?" I wasn't really sure where we were exactly. I knew in general, but I was too high to have kept up with exactly how far down 31 we had gone.

"No, not far now." She was slowing, then turned down a dirt road. I saw the road sign that read Constant Church Road.

"She went to Constant Church?" I asked.

"That's what Lily and Mike said she had planned. To go out there and look for that 'Kerny' guy. Guess she heard about the ghost."

Constant Church was an abandoned church, one of those small congregations that just fell apart when their last preacher had died. The county looked after it, mostly due to the graveyard there. It wasn't really old, just small and out of the way. And somehow a story about it being haunted started up, prolly because it was weird in Jubal County to not have some other church just move right in. The county loves its churches.

"I used to come out here some when I was younger. Good, quiet place to fool around. Me and my fiancé, we liked coming out this way. Used to live sorta nearby."

"Oh, I didn't know you were engaged . . ." Anna said.

"*Was*. Not anymore. It was before I dated your sister."

She nodded. I just watched the road in the headlights. I spotted the small turnoff for the church about the same time as she began to slow the car. It was overgrown, but there was still a bit of dirt road left leaving off to the right. Anna threaded the car between the ditch to either side and then the church came into sight.

It was a cinderblock building that had once been painted white. Most of the paint had worn off, and its tin roof was beginning to badly rust in spots. The grass hadn't been cut around it in months, clearly, if at all that year, and you could no longer see the small gravel spot where the cars had parked. The front door was cracked open pretty wide, and I could see a couple of the windows had been busted out. Clearly the fine youth of Jubal County had discovered the place at some point.

You couldn't see it, but I could hear the gravel crunch under the tires as Anna pulled up. She killed the car and put in park but left the headlights on. The headlights shone right in the open front door, and looking inside I could see broken pews and moldy carpet amongst the shadows.

She rolled her window down and the sounds of the night flowed in. Cicadas, crickets, and even the odd frog from the sounds of things. We sat there in silence for a few minutes, neither of us wanting to break the spell.

I was impressed. Most folks would have said something by this point. It's rare to find someone who can enjoy the silence.

Without saying anything, she cut off the headlights and stepped out of the car. I followed along after, watching her as she walked to the front of the car and sat on the hood. She sat there, looking up at the stars.

"I can see why y'all came out here," she whispered.

The way the moon was shining you could see fairly well, and it lit up her face faintly. She was all of a sudden really pretty. Really, really pretty.

I walked over, standing right in front of her between the gap in her legs. We were close—mighty close. She looked down from the stars and stared into my face. Seated on the hood like that, we were now the same height, finally face-to-face.

She leaned forward and kissed me.

Then things got a bit heated. But y'all don't need to see all that.

Sometime Around Midnight

I was sitting on the hood of the car, the light of a cigarette casting a red glow over my shirtless body. In front of me, Anna was refastening her bra.

"So *that* happened," she laughed.

I smirked. "So it did."

"Man, I used to have the biggest crush on you when you were dating my sister." She laughed, somewhat incredulously. "To finally hook up with you . . . well, you just fulfilled a little fantasy of mine."

The idea of being anyone's teenage fantasy struck me as so funny that I almost fell off the hood laughing. "Well, happy to oblige," I managed to choke out.

Tugging her shirt back on, she gave me a playful shove and then hopped up on the hood. "So now what? Do we look for clues or something?"

I shook my head. "She wasn't here. Or if she was, this isn't where she went missing, I don't reckon." I took one last pull on the cigarette. "The cops around here ain't exactly the best, but if there was a lead around here, I think they would have found it. But if I had to guess, she did go missing somewhere near here—somewhere within a few miles."

"Why do you say that?"

I sighed. "She was hunting a god. If she wanted it bad enough, she'd find one, or something similar. Though like as not, not the one she was looking for."

I paused. I'd just had a real good moment, and I didn't want to mess that up by going too deep. But maybe I owed her a better explanation than I would usually give. Breathing out a cloud of smoke, weighing my options in the second it provided, I carried on. "See, most folks ain't got the belief. Not really, though they think they do. Most folks, they naturally avoid places where the real supernatural is. It's second nature to them—keeps them safe. Prolly some sort of evolutionary defense or something. But if you really believe, or iff'n you get exposed to it somehow then, well, you can get drawn to shit you shouldn't be."

I could feel her staring at me. "You're serious, aren't you?"

I nodded.

She sat there for a minute not saying anything. Finally, she spoke. "Ok."

"Ok?"

She looked at me, giving a little shrug. "Ok."

"Fair enough," I said with a slight smile.

She stood up, facing me, jingling her keys at me. "So again, what now? We going god hunting?"

I slid off the hood. "WE are riding back to my shed and are going to get well and truly fucked up. Then, when you can, YOU are going home. Then I am going to go find her."

She leaned over and kissed me. Her lips tasted of sweat and smoke, and it was perfect. She winked at me. "We'll see."

I grinned. "I guess we will. Now I gotta take a leak—be right back."

She laughed. "Ever the romantic, Marsh. But me too; I'm going around behind my car." She looked at me hard then. "You peek and I will leave you out here."

I was already walking to go behind the church. "Fair!" I said over my shoulder.

It was darker behind the church.

Reaching into my pants I pulled out my wallet, thumbing through it until I found a small picture. Holding it between my fingers, I began muttering some words under my breath, my eyes squeezed tightly shut. I could feel my high fading fast as the energy pulsed through my fingertips.

When I opened them, a silvery shadow was in front of me. A little PT Cruiser, all misty and indistinct, with two people standing beside it looking up, holding hands. I stared at it for a bit till it faded away. I tucked the picture away and walked back to the car.

Anna was leaning against the driver side door. "Took you long enough. Must have taken you awhile to find it."

"You know that's a lie," I smirked.

"I guess I do," she laughed, climbing into the car.

SHE SELLS SANCTUARY

The rising sun woke me, its bright rays filtering into my shed through the half-open roll-up door. I was lying in my recliner, arm wrapped around Anna, who was curled up against my chest. Her long limbs were covered in just a T-shirt, and her skin lay warm against my own. I didn't remember a lot of what happened after we got to my shed, but the flashes I could were druggy magic.

I sat up a bit, propping myself up on my elbow. I could see that Anna was so tall that her feet were hanging off the foot of the recliner just a little. And that the shirt she had one was one of mine. Her clothes and mine were scattered about the room. All in all, it had been a good night.

A damn good night.

I thought of trying to ease out from under her without waking her, but it was far too small a space for that. She stirred, and with a back-arching yawn she turned and looked me in the eye. I would have looked at her back, but that stretch had caused the shirt to ride up, revealing that was the only thing she had on. Turns out a shirt meant for me was a bit short on her. Delightfully so.

My hand starting creeping in interesting directions, which she let happen. She laid back and closed her eyes. "Your hands are rough," she muttered, biting her lip a little.

They were indeed heavily calloused from time spent doing farm work. "Been living hard," I said by way of excuse.

"I like it," she whispered, her back arching once more.

When we finished, I stood up from the cot and set about finding my pants. She just sat in the recliner, wearing nothing but a thin sheen of sweat and a slight, happy smile. I nodded toward the open doorway. "That don't bother you?"

She looked over at it as though seeing it for the first time. She gave a small shrug. "If it doesn't bother you, it doesn't bother me."

I shuffled into my pants. "Fair enough."

She stretched languidly, looking up at the ceiling. "So what are we doing today? Gonna go find Angie?"

I started rummaging around through the detritus of my home, mining for some smokes. " 'We'? I'm thinking *you'll* get dressed and ride on, return to normal life. Me, I'll sit around a bit, eat a Pop-Tart, do some drugs, then scrounge up a ride. That's what I'm thinking."

Anna laughed. "Right. So where do you think she is? Where are we going to start?"

My eyebrow raised. "Didn't you hear me just then?"

She sat up on the bed, turning so that her feet were on the floor. "Cards on the table, Marsh. Last night was amazing. At least the moments I can remember clearly." She gave a little shake of pleasure, her eyes rolling back just a little. "I'm single. You're single. We have fun together. During the week I have school and work. But on the weekends, I want to hang. Why scrounge up a ride when you have a ride right here?" She cupped her small chest and winked. "Pun intended."

"Fucking puns," I laughed. I eyed her over, though. There was something about her. I sat there silent, considering. She proceeded to start finding her clothes.

She had a sense of self, it seemed. Like she knew who she was, what she wanted. Which, while not rare, was at least a bit uncommon among folks our age. She was normal, of course, but other than that, she was like me—well, other than being like a foot taller. Which, now that I wasn't as high, didn't seem quite as tall. And I had been right: The physics of it last night *had* been fun.

There was a moral question, though. I'd likely already brought her a bit too far into my world. But if I hadn't, did I have the right to take her any further? I decided I didn't, really; we'd have to go our separate ways, at least for today.

And then she bent over right in front of me to pull her panties on.

"What the hell," I said, pulling her onto my lap.

THE LONG AND WINDING ROAD

Each of us munching on a Pop-Tart, we made our way down the road. She'd given me shit about my paltry pantry selection, but I just ignored it. I mostly ate food that had been packaged and sealed outside the county, shit like Spam and Little Debbie snack cakes. It wasn't the healthiest of diets, but considering the poison I put into my body on the daily, that was the least of my worries, I reckoned. An overdose would kill me long before heart disease got to me.

I had dug out a CD from my collection to replace her musical selection. So now instead of some sort of Norwegian black metal, the heavy tones of Crowbar were filling the air. It wasn't cranked quite as loud as last night, either, being quiet enough that we could more easily talk.

Turns out Anna was cool with weed, booze, and the odd pill. And she said she didn't mind me using meth, though

I was pretty sure I saw a little tinge of worry there as she said it. She just wouldn't partake. So I was fairly humming along, and I imagined the couple of pills she had taken had her feeling rather grand herself.

We were headed back in the general direction of Constant Church. My gut was telling me that was the right direction, and I knew better than to ignore my gut. The girl had gone god hunting and had decided that haunted places were her best bet. So there had to be something in the vicinity of the church.

Well, actually, there was certainly something in the vicinity of the church; there is something in the vicinity of everywhere. I didn't have a handle on all the theology, but it was pretty clear to me that in the cracks of the world, energies got caught up. Some called them gods, some angels, some devils. I had a thought that maybe they changed to fit the person looking. But it's not like there are books lying around on the subject. Or if there are, they didn't make it to the Elk Grove Library.

I thought for a bit more. "Go to the church first. I reckon she made it that far."

"Yeah?" she asked.

"Yeah. I met the girl once, and my read on her was not a good one. I reckon she showed up there pissy about her friends doing their own thing that night. Then she got out there, and nothing happened, so she got even pissier.

Prolly thinking to herself how bad she wants to have something happen so she can show up her friends, make them jealous. She finally got to wanting it bad enough. So something happened."

Anna was quiet for a minute. "What do you think happened?"

"It's been six months. She's dead." I thought a second. "Or if she ain't, she's wishing she was."

"Not very optimistic there, Marsh," she said.

I gave a little half smile. "Life's taught me better, I suppose." I could feel the faint sniff of sad thoughts starting to twitter around the edges of my mind. Couldn't have that, so I started thinking other thoughts. "But hey, maybe she just got, got by a run-of-the-mill serial killer or something!"

Anna looked over at me for a second, then gave an exasperated laugh. "Damn it, Marsh." She reached over and snaked her hand into mine, giving it a little squeeze before returning it to the wheel.

The twittering stopped. And the growing high started wrapping itself around me in its warm, energetic embrace. I was getting ready to get up out this car and do some traipsing around.

Looking out the window I saw we were getting pretty close. We actually passed by my old house, though I didn't mention it. Then I saw the purple car.

Set off from the road, it was some sort of Civic or the like and bright purple with matte black rims. Parked out in an abandoned field where about ten years ago there had been a house. It dawned on me, as it did every time I saw that purple car, that I should investigate it. There was something weird about a car just sitting out like that. But I always seemed to forget about it soon as it got out of sight . . .

We turned down the dirt road Constant Church resided upon, and a few minutes later we were sitting in its driveway once again. Anna put the car in park and looked over at me expectantly. "Now what?"

I thought for a second. "Well, I never much made it past Constant Church on this road that I can recall. I don't rightly know where it even goes. And if I don't, you can bet Angie didn't, not being from around here. She was off hunting adventure, so it seems to me that adventure is more likely to be down the road less travelled."

Anna put the car in drive and pulled back onto the dirt road.

"Now this may sound weird, but I want you to tell me everything of note that you see," I said.

"What do you mean 'of note'?" she asked.

"Basically anything except trees and trash alongside the road. If you see it, call it out. And drive slow, so as you don't miss anything, if you please."

She looked at me for a moment, clearly thinking to ask more, but instead pressed down on the gas. She obliged with my request, though. We set off down that road, which had thankfully been grated and graveled somewhat recently, her calling out what she saw.

It was fairly typical fare for Jubal County. We passed what had to be a hunting camp, consisting of an old camper with a few logs set around a fire ring. A couple of tree stands leaned up against its side, which told me exactly how much travel this road got, as those were prime stealing material. If I could find a truck to borrow, they'd be snatched and sold in a week.

A bit farther on she called out a mailbox, and dutifully she mentioned the ratty trailer that it stood sentinel over. It was rough looking, with a mountain of trash and crushed beer cans littering the yard. The rusted hulk of some sort of old truck leered out from the tree line at the edge of the yard as well. All in all, a dismal sort of place that I was pretty sure was unoccupied currently. Though the way things worked in the county, someone's broke cousin or some meth cook would move in before too much longer.

The sights rolled slowly past. A small beaver pond that abutted the road, a place where folks had taken to dumping old mattresses and appliances, a couple of small drives without mailboxes that led back to who knows what. Each was called out by Anna as it came into sight.

Rounding a curve, I could see the end of the road up ahead about a quarter mile up with what looked at this distance to be some old house all overgrown with vines and the like.

"Alright, I see the end of the road. Guess that's it. I can stop now?" Anna asked from behind the wheel.

I paused. Maybe she hadn't noticed the house because of all the vines. But we got closer and she still didn't mention it. "The end of the road . . . that's all you see?"

She slowed the car to a stop and sat there for a minute, looking more closely. We couldn't be more than forty yards from the house at this point. Even though it was set back off from the road a bit, there was no way she didn't see it. "Ok, I give, what am I missing?" she asked.

I pointed. "There is a house there, to the right. Off, back from the road about thirty feet. Brick and wood, covered in vines. See it?"

She stared hard where I was pointing, and I saw her eyes widen. "Oh, weird, how did I miss that?"

"Because your brain was trying to protect you." We had found a spot. Maybe not *the* spot, but a spot. One of the cracks in the world. "I think this might be the spot. So if you would, park up there nearby and stay inside. Keep the car running, though, in case I have to run."

She shook her head. "I think I would rather go in with you. I mean, I came this far. And I can just leave the car running."

"You don't know what you are saying," I said, cracking my knuckles nervously. Between the joys my box of oblivion had wrought on me and my anxiousness, I was suddenly wound up tight as a coil. I undid my seatbelt and leaned forward, craning my neck to look at the house closer. "Don't know at all."

The house looked to be about thirty years old or so. The first couple of feet up from the ground it was brick, then it turned to some sort of wooden siding. It had been painted blue, it looked like, though most of the paint was gone. All the windows were intact, save for one which a limb had fallen through. All over it grew vines and creepers, most of them poisonous by the look of them. They were so thick in places that you couldn't even see the house, growing over it like a shaggy coat of fur.

"Hey, you've trusted me this far," she was saying.

My knuckles had all been cracked, but I kept trying them out of reflex. I was humming at about an eleven, a ball of nervous, manic energy needing to explode outwards. I looked at her. "Let's deal. I'm going in. If it's safe enough, I'll wave you in."

She nodded slowly. "You promise?"

"Yeah," I mumbled hastily.

"Can I trust your promises?"

That was a thorny question. In general, no. A man is only as good as his word, but then I am not a very good man. I mean, I generally *intended* to keep a good half of my promises, maybe even a bit more than that, but things tended to get in the way. I looked at her, though, and it clicked a little.

"You can. You. Today. Maybe not tomorrow. But fuck it. Right now, YOU can." Damn, I wanted out of that car. I needed to stretch my legs, my body.

She held out her hand, pinky extended. "I'm going to hold you to it, Marsh."

I looked at her hand a little incredulously but followed suit. We entwined pinkies. "I promise. Can I go now, Mom?"

She rolled her eyes. "Get the fuck out, Marsh."

I practically flew out the door.

Up Into Roses

I had forgotten how humid it had been. Riding around in air conditioning will do that to you, spoil you against the heat. By the time I had the door shut, I swear sweat was already starting to bead up on me. The air was so thick it was about like walking through a warm fog.

Besides that, though, there was an energy in the air. It wasn't as in-your-face as the humidity but if you were in tune with such shit, as I was, it was clearly there. As clearly as the heat, the sun, and the slowly dying house in front of me. It was like a static charge in the air, as though I had been shuffling my feet across one of my aunt's shag carpets all morning.

I sort of paced side to side for a minute, eyeing that house over. If I hadn't been all tweaked out, maybe I could have just stood and stared. Not so, though—I was way too fucked up for that. It honestly wasn't a real good feeling, but that ship had long sailed.

Nothing seemed to be moving, least not that I could see. The surroundings were overgrown, of course, the forest that had once bordered the yard having fully invaded in the years since the original inhabitants had moved out. I looked around for any sort of clue as to what I might be dealing with, but nothing stood out to me. And frankly, I had run out of patience to keep looking.

I strode up what would have once been the driveway, leading to a carport big enough for just one car. I could see a few moldy boxes and a couple of rusted-up kids' bikes, but other than that there was nothing of note. I decided against pawing through the boxes. There might be some good loot, but this might end up a crime scene, and it wouldn't do to have too many fingerprints just lying around.

A rusted screen door led into the house, so taking the hem of my shirt, I used it to grab the door handle and let myself inside. It groaned a bit but opened readily enough. A small shower of rust flecks rained down, shook loose from the screen, to fall on my shoes. Ignoring that, I stepped in.

There was magic thick in the air. I could feel it washing over me, taking the place of the humidity. I was standing in what had been the kitchen, but everything was bathed in a pale-green light, as though the windows had been green tinted glass instead of the dirt-smudged panes they actually were. Vines had covered the window, but that in no way explained the verdant tinge to the room's color.

The linoleum had curled, peeling back in places, and in those spots thick tufts of grass had grown up, which, to my mind, should not have really been possible. A trio of jet-black butterflies were fluttering around the room, making languid circles.

There was a sickly sweet scent in the air. It was like someone had Febreezed a corpse and had almost done a good enough job. It was enough to make my nose crinkle, and I got to thinking it might be a better idea to just dip out.

Fuck my curiosity.

I stepped in, letting the screen door ease closed behind me. A snuffling sound reached my ear. It was hard to pinpoint, but it sounded like a fat man trying to breathe through a bad sinus attack. It was an almost familiar sound . . . something was playing around the edge of my memory, threatening to be remembered. But when I was wired up like this it was hard to think right, hard to make those connections, dredge up those memories.

Two doors led out of the kitchen. The one to my right went into what must have been the laundry room or some sort of glorified pantry. Straight ahead there appeared to be either a dining room or the start of a living room.

Whatever it was, it was even more overgrown than the kitchen.

My body, having had enough of just standing around, seemingly got a mind of its own and before I was even fully aware of what I was doing, I had made my way across the room. Striding into what proved to be a large living room, my march came to a crashing halt as I ran into its occupant. "Shit."

"Marsh, why, it's been some time, hasn't it?" The voice was deep and lugubrious, vibrating with a thickly phlegmy quality.

I had stumbled into the new home of the King.

A grossly fat satyr lay sprawled across a dirty mattress. His fur was dirty and matted, and from twenty feet away I could see the bugs crawling through it. Raising his head up from a pile of what may have at one time been pillows, the King propped himself up on his elbow. His skin was jaundiced and covered with oozing sores, each secreting purplish puss.

Trying not to retch, I gave a bow. "Your Majesty," I said through gritted teeth.

What exactly he was King of had never been made clear to me. But when dealing with the things between the cracks of reality, it was always the best move to go with what they claimed. Our two previous run-ins had ended . . .

neutrally. The sort of neutral where both parties walk away unhappy, and both know it. Had I known the King was involved, I would have just kept well enough away. Third time's a charm, they say, but I am a firm believer that luck tends to side with the more powerful, and if he really wanted to, the King could probably swat me like a gnat.

The King staggered to his feet with much grunting, his bulk rocking to and fro. He was so tall that his horns brushed the ceiling, and glancing up I could see that plaster there had been scored countless times by them. He slipped a finger into one of his sores. Coating his finger with the goo, he slipped it into his mouth with an odious slurping sound. His eyes rolled back a bit and he shuddered. As he came down from his pleasure rush, he looked to me once more. "Little Marsh. What brings you into my kingdom this day?"

The sorrow in his voice was palpable. I had a suspicion that whatever depression had him in its hold was the reason I had survived so far. Sad gods are easier to deal with than angry gods. Safer, at least, for a time.

I kept my head down, which was a huge struggle. My natural contrariness was rising up within me, and the host of drugs pumping through my system were not helping to calm me down. Choking back my natural snarkiness while I still could, I spoke. "My King, I am looking for a young woman who may have visited you."

"We do not get many visitors to our glorious realm anymore," snuffed the King.

In truth, it was rather pretty in there. The subtle magics that followed every step the King took had caused the room to grow into a riot of beautiful greens as nature reclaimed the room. Save for the foul mattress, most of the room may as well have been outside, or perhaps in a mossy cave. Fluorescent azure mushrooms dotted the walls, adding a blue tint to the greenish glow of the air.

Fat fingers swiped at the wall as the King plucked a dark-red rose from the wall and plopped it into his mouth. It began to regrow immediately, this time a violet color. Munching his treasure with lip-smacking chews, blood-red juices flowing down his chins, he continued. "So it was a happy day when our last visitors came. There were two women and a man—perhaps one of them is who you seek."

I started. "Was this about a half a year ago, Your Majesty?"

The King snuffled. "What is time but an illusion?" he sighed. "So long, so long. It has been like this ever since I was forced to move." He looked to me, his eyes brimming with tears. "I am so alone now, thanks to you."

I was a major reason as to why he had been forced to relocate, though in truth he brought it on himself, as he well knew. Still, the King could hold a grudge.

"I still feel bad about that, I promise you." I didn't, of course, but it pays to be cautious.

The King snorted, his fat belly wobbling obscenely as he did. Idly he reached down into the trail of fur that grew upon his stomach, pulling out a fat, bloated tick. He flicked it into this mouth and gave a little shudder of pleasure. I had to fight to not throw up. Luckily, he spoke, distracting me enough to keep my mind from that little horror. "They were here, we feasted, we entertained by the pond, but some have left and that day is past. What more need be said?" He turned away from me. "You, too, may leave now."

I blanched inwardly. The King's feasts never ended well. A creature like the King, he fed on the emotions of people around him. The more negative, the better. He himself rarely directly killed anything. But someone hopped up on one of his feasts, they could—and would—do whatever their basest emotions and instincts told them to do. I had been to one. I knew. I still cringe to think about what happened that night, and I have seen some shit.

I had been dismissed, so I figured to make a bowing escape while the whimsical, somewhat good mood of the King held.

And then a car door shut outside.

The King perked up. "Oh, Marsh, did you bring a friend?"

All Hail the King

The King was loathe to directly interfere with me, as I bore the mark of another. But anyone around me, well, they would be fair game.

I eyed the monster warily. "I had someone drive me here, yeah."

A faint smile fought through the sadness drawn on his face. "Well why haven't you introduced them to us? I just told you how lonely it was here."

I walked over to the window, cursing inwardly. Peering through the vines that were growing over it, I could see that Anna had gotten out and was leaning against her door smoking a cigarette. I breathed a sigh of relief. I thought she was coming in, but I should have known she'd have a bit more sense than that.

"My King, let me just go get them." I would just walk out, climb in the car, and we would be off. Easy peasy.

"No. Call to them—they'll hear. We don't trust you, little Marsh."

Shit. I looked out the window, then back to the satyr. His face was growing red, anger bulling away the sorrow. I had to do something quick.

Well, I had all this energy. May as well use it.

I opened my mouth as though to yell while my right hand, which was blocked from his view by my body, began making a series of intricate swirling motions. I could feel the power well up within me, my lungs expanding painfully.

I turned my head toward the King and loosed a roar.

Power tore through me, fueled by the array of drugs in my system. Far more powerful than what I could have achieved on my own, a toxic wind of foul breath slammed into the creature, staggering him backwards. Purple pus splattered from his gaping sores as the satyr fought to keep his footing. Around him the verdant scene began to wilt and turn brown, unable to cope with my unnatural source of energy.

I'm poison, and this just proved it.

I had nowhere near enough strength to fight the King; I just needed to stagger him a moment. So clamping my mouth shut, I turned and sprinted for the kitchen door, my ratty boots tearing up the clumps of grass that dotted the way.

Behind me the King roared with anger and came barreling after me. I could hear his hooves slamming against the floor as he powered forward just a dozen feet behind me. I glanced back just in time to see him slam into the doorway that separated the kitchen from his bedroom. His bulk was such that he tore through the doorway, knocking a massive chunk from the portal with his shoulders as he forced his way past it. His eyes were blood red now, his mouth foaming.

In truth, I was lucky he was so pissed. If he was less angry, he might have remembered he had powers that could likely stop me in my tracks.

I sprinted through the screen door, shouting as I went, "Get in the car! Get in the car!"

Coming from under the carport I saw her clambering in behind the wheel. Behind me, the King had reached the screen door. Luckily for me, the entryway there was brick and metal, not wood and plaster, so he was having to squeeze his bulk through gradually, which further slowed him. He was raging incoherently, an unending string of invectives slurring from his foaming mouth.

Anna had flung open my door and I all but dove inside. "Drive, drive!!!" I screeched.

Her eyes were wide as she caught sight of the King, who was almost through the door, his sides red with blood as he tore his flesh on the too-tight doorway. "What the fuck . . ."

I grabbed her face. Locking eyes with her, I demanded, "Fucking *go!*"

Shaking, she turned back to the wheel and slammed it into drive. She punched the gas so hard that for a moment the tires just spun in the dirt. It wasn't till the tires caught and we lunged forward that I realized that I had been holding my breath. Letting it out with a ragged cough, I looked to our right.

The King had made it out the door and was thundering down the short drive. Anna had hooked the wheel and was turning us in a tight circle to get us pointed up the dirt road and away from the creature. Looking from our progress to the King, I had a powerful suspicion that we were not going to make it.

Anna had the car on the road proper now and gave it all she had to get us moving up and away. The King was on the other side of the car from me now, and for a moment I lost sight of him. I craned my neck frantically, trying to pick him back up again. Then my head slammed into the side window so hard I thought I cracked my skull.

The King had rammed the back right panel, right around the trunk area. His curved horns had slammed into the car with enough force to send us sideways, and briefly up on two wheels. Anna screamed, or maybe I did—hell, maybe we both did. It was pretty crazy at that moment, too crazy to go tracking down the source of every little scream that filled the air.

Trying to blink away the pain, I looked behind us. The King was still coming after us, and unless Anna got on that gas, he might well catch us. It was sorta like that scene in Jurassic Park where the T. rex goes tearing after that Jeep. I could see that one of his horns had cracked, which I was sure did nothing to improve his mood. He was gnashing his teeth at the air in between rage-choked bellows, destruction clearly foremost on his mind.

I saw his muscles tense for a moment, and then he leapt. I lost sight of him as he sprung over the car. I was so shocked that something so fat could even attempt any-thing of the sort that I was struck dumb. I whipped my head around and tried to say a warning when the creature landed in front of the car, head lowered.

With a deafening yell Anna snatched the wheel and swerved left. The satyr's broken horn sheared off my side mirror and from the sounds of things left a deep score down the side of the car. But then we were past.

I looked back, but the King seemed to have given up his pursuit, taking out his rage by violently attacking a nearby tree with his huge fists. Then we rounded the curve, going way too fast, and he was out of sight.

"It's ok, he stopped chasing us," I said, slumping tiredly into my seat.

Anna slowed to a slightly safer speed, though her breathing was still fast. "What the fuck was that?!" she asked, panic hovering at the edge of her voice.

I reached out my hand, and put it on her thigh. "Hey, you did real good back there."

She pushed my hand off and started to crane her head to try and see the damage. "Not too damn good. My car is fucked, it looks like," she said, looking in her side mirror. "Fuck me."

I forced a smile, though I certainly wasn't feeling it. "I wouldn't worry about that. I got some money coming. I know where Angie is, so that reward money's mine. I'll fix the car."

"Where is she?" Anna asked, her panicked voice calming fractionally, replaced with a hint of curiosity.

I figured if I would keep talking, keep her at least a little distracted, that might keep the panic at bay. "Well, she's either dead or a prisoner of the King back there. I think Mike and Lily lied; they were with her the night she went looking. They went hunting Cernunnos but found the King instead. He likes to party, and he would have made them join him in a feast. Things probably got real, real weird. Like . . . sex weird."

A thought came to me. "Mike and Lily—I bet they used to not be the kind of folks who would fuck in the mud under a bridge. Least not till about six months ago. Am I right?"

Anna nodded slowly, her eyes hooding. She was pissed but listening. "Mike, he was straight edge. No sex, no drinking, no . . . anything. Then, out of the blue, they started shacking up every chance they could get."

"It's the lingering effect of the King's magic. They probably don't really remember anything. Their minds are trying to protect them, but once you feast with a satyr, it takes a while to shake the effect. Angie was probably in heaven." I shuddered at the thought, remembering the tick. "He told me three people had visited but 'some' left. Which means 'some' didn't. And we know who made it out. So the question is if Angie's alive or dead."

We'd reached the end of the dirt road. Anna stopped, and turning, she looked at me. "Could she be . . ."

I shrugged. "It's possible. I've heard the King has been known to take a servant in the past. But I don't want you to get your hopes up. Like as not, she died during the feast." I decided now was not the time to mention that had that happened, her friends would very likely have feasted on her flesh. "At least that's my highly educated guess. Not that they will remember having done it, most likely."

Anna glanced at me, her mouth open to speak. Then she closed it and turned back to the road. She didn't say anything till we made it back to the U-Store-It, which I took as a mighty bad sign. It was a damn shame, as I had quickly grown rather fond of her. She had stones, that was for sure.

As we pulled up in front of my home, she put the car in park and looked over at me. She sat there in silence for a minute as though she was weighing me out.

"What?" I asked after an uncomfortable minute. I hated talks like this; I would much rather get it over with so I could go ahead and just get fucked up.

"Hell of a second date, Marsh." She reached over and slipped her hand into mine. "Maybe the third date, though, we just go get some food."

"What? After that, you still want to . . . even after all that?" I asked, jerking my thumb behind me.

She shrugged. "I won't lie, that was maybe the most scared I've ever been in my life. And let me be real fucking clear, I never want to encounter anything like that again. But I asked for it, even after you tried warning me off. Now I know a little better, know that when you say I don't want to know or see something, maybe I should listen."

I nodded slowly, not really allowing myself to believe her, much as I wanted to.

"And let's be real," she carried on. "We aren't anything serious. We have fun together, last half hour being the exception. I have my life, you have yours, and they've got to stay separate for the most part, I think. But come the weekends . . ." She gave a weak smile. "Come the weekends, I think I would like to keep hanging out."

"Ok, then," I said. She was right—I had sorta been getting ahead of myself in my own mind, even if I hadn't said anything aloud. She was fun, but all I knew about her really was that she seemed into me, which typically didn't speak too well of folks. I ran my tongue over the few teeth I had left. Folks with a full mouth of shiny white didn't typically settle down with someone with more missing than present.

"That's fair. No more hoodoo." I drew my finger across my heart in an X. "Cross my heart."

She snorted, turning my other hand loose. "So, next weekend. Food. Me. You. Cool?"

"Cool," I grinned.

She kissed me then. "At least you're not boring. Can't stand a boring guy. Now get out of my poor battered car, I have places to be."

Still a little incredulous, I stepped out. "I'll help get it fixed," I offered as a parting gift.

"Deal. Now bye, Marsh," she said through the open window. "See you Friday."

I was pretty sure she had started to cry a little. I wasn't sure if the stress had hit her and she was freaking out, or . . . hell, I didn't know. I know I felt like crying. I was still standing there bewildered when her taillights disappeared off down the road.

PLOTTING

Popping the last bite of Spam Single into my mouth, I wiped my hands on my jeans. Around a mouthful of poor man's steak, I carried on. "Bastard fucked her car up bad, but not so bad we couldn't get out of there in a hurry. Then she dropped me off, and here I am."

HD was leaned against the doorway of my shed, listening intently to my tale. I'd called him in because I knew I was gonna need a ride soon, but more importantly, I needed someone in the know to bounce ideas off of. He'd done good, listening without interrupting me every five seconds with annoying questions like most folks would have.

"Been awhile since the King pulled a stunt like this," he said after a few moments of thought. He snuffed the nub of his cigarette out on the heel of his boot, then flicked the butt into the gravel. "Do you think she's alive?"

I shook my head. "He was acting all sad and mopey, all lonely like. So my guess is she's dead. But who knows for how long?"

"True. Need some sort of proof, though, one way or the other."

I frowned. I'd known it, had been thinking it, but to hear it said out loud . . .

"Yeah, I know it. I was hoping somehow to avoid that. Seeing as how bad I pissed him off, I don't want to be anywhere near there. But it's gotta be done."

"Telling the cops ain't the way, not yet. Best case, they get pissed at you for a wild goose chase; worst case, a couple of them end up dead."

I decided to keep my thoughts to myself on exactly how bad it would be if one or two of my tormentors ran into the King. HD was a bit more partial to the law than me, having had considerably fewer run-ins with them over the years. "They wouldn't even see the place, not without me there to point it out. And if I'm there . . . well, the King was sorta 'live and let live' on me before. Now, though, he'd probably not even slow down as he trampled the sheriff to get at me."

"I could maybe try talking to your granny about it," HD offered, his voice neutral.

"Why, so she can just tell you to tell me to handle it? If she'd wanted that girl found, she'd have done it by now. You know she ain't stepping out that house without it benefiting her in some way." There was absolutely no love lost between us, but like the rest of the family, I was held good and in check by fear. "Unless she's got a mind to go after the reward."

My uncle snorted. Granny cared not one whit for money, least it seemed like. She was probably sitting on a fuck-tall pile of it, anyways, from all the little "favors" she did folks.

"She might know something might would help, though," he said a moment later.

I looked him dead in the eye, my gaze as blank as I could make it. "And she's suddenly gonna break twenty years of tradition and actually try and teach me something?"

He lowered his gaze, sighing. "Point."

"So, look, she ain't gonna help—not unless we can think of some way to convince her, which I doubt. So let's think about what we can do to keep me alive, iff'n the King walks up while I'm sneaking around looking." I walked over to my little minifridge and pulled out my last two beers. They weren't terribly cold—my fridge was a little busted, but they would do in a pinch. I handed one to HD. "So put your thinking cap on. He's bigger, stronger, and faster. Keep me alive."

"Well—" he started. I cut him off first.

"And keep in mind, I wasn't going quite full blast, but I damn near gave him my best shot and all it managed to do was knock him back a step or two for about a second. It did a better job of pissing him off than doing anything to hurt him. So if you are thinking any sort of spell I can muster, well, you're outside your mind. 'Less you know something I don't."

It was frustrating, to say the least. I had no doubt that out there somewhere were better spells, something that could actually hurt the bastard, or maybe some way of upping my juice without getting so hopped up on meth that I couldn't sit still for a split second. There was power in my blood—old power, ancient power, but without any real idea how to use it, I was left cobbling together the little dribs and drabs I had.

Being supremely lazy didn't much help either. My motivation to learn left me around the same time I lost my teacher all those decades ago, and it showed.

"Well," he said archly, eyeing me to see if I aimed to interrupt again, "only one thing comes immediately to mind. It won't keep you alive long, but it might buy you enough time to get someplace safer. Though just where that might be, I haven't a clue."

I looked at him expectantly. "Yes?"

He grinned at me. "How are you coming along on practicing your glyphs?"

I glanced over to my dry erase board, which was covered in dust and tucked up in a pile of treasure. "Fuck."

Crash Course

H D just kept lecturing away, driving me to distraction. I would have maybe paid attention except for two things. First, it wasn't anything I hadn't already heard before at length. Second, the bastard was right, and I just couldn't stand to hear "I told you so."

Should I have been practicing my glyphs and sigils? Yes. I knew that, he clearly knew that, everyone knew that. He'd been after me for years now to really get after them, to stop wasting my time. But a few months back I had almost gotten serious and had even scooped up a dry erase board to practice on from the back of the Christian Mission.

But then . . . well, life got in the way. Not in any real way, I suppose, but I'd be fucked if I could find the motivation. As HD kept on chattering away I made a promise to myself: After tonight I would get serious about learning the shit. If for no other reason than to not have to sit through this particular string of lecturing word vomit.

I might even keep on it.

Leaning back in my recliner, my job was minimal. I just had to lay there with my shirt off as my uncle started to paint on me. As he painted, I had to feed a trickle of my power into the glyphs to power them. Not too much, since I wasn't the one drawing them up, or else they could backfire in a bad way onto HD.

"It all starts with the spiral," he was saying as he dipped the brush into the yellow paint. Pulling it out, he began to paint a slow, steady swirl, the start of which began in the center of my chest. "All power comes from the spiral and returns there when it's spent. And if you draw it just right, every other glyph will be that much stronger for it."

I was lucky my chest was hairless, so the paint went smoothly onto my flesh. It wasn't just a spiral, of course—I mean not some random one you could just throw on all willy-nilly. It had a particular number of swirls and had to line up just so and all that. The spiral was the one glyph I knew. I could glance up on my back wall where the old deer skull hung, painted black and bearing the yellow spiral on it. It would be an exact mirror of the one on my chest when HD was finished.

Lots of times, magic—it skips a generation. Especially when two powerful spellslingers like my grandparents hook up. I guess to prevent someone being born who was just too powerful. Not that magic has to make any sense, I guess. But it had mostly skipped my parents' generation, only to breed true in mine.

HD had no magic, none that he could actually use, but the subject ate at him, I knew. He had himself a little collection of books, though Lord knows where he got them, and he studied over them regularly. It made him the biggest expert I knew that would actually talk to me about it. Obviously Granny knew more, far more, but she'd made it damn clear she was never gonna teach me shit.

I wondered, not for the first time, if Granny knew about HD's little obsession and his tiny library. My gut told me no, and I decided that some things were better left unsaid. Which could also be said for pretty much ninety percent of my family history.

"I've heard some folks now'days are getting the spiral tattooed on them. Even some glyphs. It's dangerous, of course, but if it holds, the payoff would be incredible, I think. You could look into it maybe, though you couldn't use any of your scratcher buddies to do it. Prison ink ain't gonna get it done," he snorted.

He'd finished the first pass of the spiral and now was going over it again to make sure the lines were good and clean. I was just steadily feeding a touch of power in, and you could see the yellow glowing faintly in the trail of the brush strokes. It left an echo of pale gold if you closed your eyes.

"That's a thought," I said. I did love a tattoo, and I was pretty shit at making the glyphs myself. If I could score an easy way out . . .

"Well, we'd have to find someone who could do it, and you can bet they don't advertise that shit far and wide. So in the meantime, you need to keep . . ." And the lecturing began again.

I suddenly recalled an offer for some art lessons. Maybe I could finagle that into mastering glyphs somehow. Ms. Yasmine had offered, and I wasn't opposed to a little yard work as payment. It might keep me focused long enough to actually master something a little more complex than three swirls.

He'd moved to my left forearm, beginning work on the glyph that would go there, still prattling on. I was thinking ahead, though, about what I had to do. If the King saw me, I'd be in real trouble. I'd never acted so directly against him before, and he was infamous for holding grudges. Though in truth, those grudges often didn't last very long, as he would just kill whatever bothered him. There was little he feared that I knew of, other than Granny—but then everyone around these parts was scared of her.

And that was what I realized had me most worked up. The King might be worried that I would rat out his little shindig to her, that she might get involved. And what if Angie was still alive, and I was wrong about that? If she was, and the King was worried about my family looking to punish him, then I could bet Angie would vanish for good soon.

I looked down at my arm, where a complex bit of knot-work was appearing. "Unc, maybe we should get a move on."

TIGHTROPE

HD parked his van what I guessed was a bit over a mile from the pond. My memory wasn't perfectly clear on just how close we were, but I decided to try and err on the side of caution. It was at least half a mile past the pond to get to the house I had encountered the King at earlier that day. I didn't know how well he could hear, but I doubted he could hear an old van creeping down the dirt road from well over a mile away.

"Should I leave it running?" he asked. We were both just sitting there, gazing up the stretch of dusty yellow road.

I thought a second, then shook my head. "Get her turned around, pointed in the right direction, but maybe you should leave it off and keep a listen out. If I'm having to come a running, I'll be shouting for you to crank things up."

"Fair enough," he said. He slipped a cigarette from his pack, shaking it out with practiced ease, then passed it to me. "Burn one before you go?"

Hell yes I wanted it, but just as badly, I wanted to get this over with. I had taken a fairly phenomenal amount of drugs not long ago, and they were beginning to really start to kick in. If I didn't get up and moving, I was going to be all over the place. As it was, I wasn't doing a terribly good job holding it all together just then, my mind racing in a hundred different directions all at once. A dozen possible outcomes—none of them great—kept fighting to gain my focus. I tried to ignore them, but there is something about potential death that just catches the imagination.

I

was

real

fucking

high.

Sickeningly so.

So I just opened the door and stepped out into the steadily growing dusk. If I timed it right, I would have enough light to do a little looking around and then soon after a good bit of dark to do some creeping around in. But I needed to get a move on. Funny how life echoes life.

I was in the tree line before I was fully cognizant that I had left without saying anything. My head jerked back as I heard the tires begin to crunch slowly as HD turned the van around. My vision sagged a second, flickering to catch up.

Was I too high? Probably.

If I had misjudged things in that regard, I would know soon enough. I kept out of the hallucinogens, but most everything else in my box had been fair game. Anything that I could coax even a little power out of if I needed. If I didn't end up burning through the buzz with magic, I like as not wouldn't sleep for days.

Cicadas were droning on, far louder than any bug had a right to be, but I was thankful enough for it. I was trying to keep on the quieter side as I traipsed through the forest but I was too jerky, too frenetic. I kept stepping places I shouldn't, catching my clothes on limbs and shrubs.

It was edging into fall, or at least the faint chill in the air was saying as much. The woods were far from dead, but the brilliant greens of spring had long darkened into the emerald of summer and had been singed brown by late summer heat. The woods weren't dead, but they were dying.

You could almost see the skeletons the trees would be turning into soon buried under a thin layer of steadily crinkling leaves begging to fall to their death. A few pathfinders had already drifted into piles of amber husks in low points, beginning to form the rusty quilt that would lie thick on the ground come winter.

I was diving into the cool relief of the gloaming, greys and blacks lining up to battle the greens and browns that dominated my vision. Later there would be moonlight, but before that shadow would hold sway, for good or ill.

Where the cool air touched skin, I could feel my little arm hairs stand on end. There was an electricity in the air, in my chest, in my fingers, in the ground, in all things. I could feel the crackle of power reach from the spiral in my chest, aching to turn loose, to blend and merge with the world around me, aching painfully to be free.

I laughed then, a thing of joy and love, then clapped my hands tight over my mouth.

I was, indeed, too high. Closing my eyes, I counted to twenty. I was pretty sure my overclocked mind was counting too fast, however, so I did it a second time, then a third. My eyes opened a crack, I sorta braced myself, then slapped the fuck out my cheek. I didn't hold back, and I felt my jaw rock as my fingers cracked across my skin. Now THAT was electric.

I stood there and stared at my boots for a few more moments, taking stock, not trying to peel back the wonders of fucking nature with my drugged up brain. I dug in, pulling up some of my power. With my mind I threaded a narrow stream of tainted, drugged mana and tried bleeding it off into the glyphs. They took a little before they started to burn around the edges, a fire atop my skin. They could only hold so much, not having been made totally by me.

Did I dare risk casting a spell of some sort this close to the King? Or did I just hope that I had managed to burn through enough of the high by topping off my glyphs that I could now actually function?

After a moment's thought I decided against casting anything. It was a balancing act, and now it was time to pray I managed to keep on the tightrope.

Down on the Boardwalk

I managed to hold it together well enough from there on. I was flirting with disaster, but then that was pretty much my usual state of affairs, so at least it felt familiar. I didn't dive off into a deep well of getting lost in my surroundings, so that was an improvement, if nothing else.

The tree line ended a dozen feet from the water in a jagged line of stumps. I could see now that this was a beaver pond, judging from the gnawed remains of trees that jutted up like jagged teeth. Looking to my right I could see the jumbled mass of the dam maybe fifty yards away, rising up from the surface of the water by a few feet.

Thin wisps of mist were rising up from the water, forming a thin film across the surface. In the evening light the water was dark, almost black, and with the lack of wind it was smooth as glass. The smell of it filled the air, almost brackish, a rich odor of algae and stagnant water.

There was a small pier nearby. Its pilings on one side looked to have rotted through, and half of its length now lay as much as a foot below the water. Next to it was an old jon boat half filled with water, its rear sunken to the very edge of the water. It was hard to tell from where I stood if it was just rusted and covered in mud or if someone had painted it brown. Either way it was a squat, ugly little craft.

Trees surrounded the pond on all sides, though to my right the trees thinned and I could see the road. Looking across, my eyes drifted to about where I thought the house would be. The land rose up from the pond and the trees were thick, so I failed to find it. Which I hoped was a good thing.

The King had said they had feasted by the pond, so I hoped that I would find something soon. My eyes followed the edges of the water, looking for anything unusual, anything that might allow me to narrow my focus. I was sure I would need to be on the other side of the pond, as the King could be real fucking lazy, I knew, but it didn't hurt to be sure.

A flash of light caught my eye, a momentary flicker quick as a snap. A firefly. As I watched, it flashed again, this time joined by another. They were on the far side, across the pond, and then a good fifty yards to the left. As I stared, more and more began to flit to life, at first a handful but soon enough there were dozens, maybe a couple hundred.

They threaded into a living chain of light, swirling through the woods to wend their way along parallel to the bank. It was as though strands of flickering white Christmas lights had come to life and were levitating their way through the forest. It was a hauntingly beautiful sight, and very clearly something unnatural.

As I watched, they seemed to reach their destination. The chain became a circle, but that far away and through the growing darkness, I could not see what it was they were about. It was a large loop, though, and I had a hint that maybe there was a clearing there.

I walked over to the little pier. Looking in, I saw that the jon boat was in good shape but that some fool had left the plug in. It was filled with rainwater that had been there long enough that a generous crop of algae coated much of the boat's bottom. More importantly, though, there was a paddle lying in the bottom.

Reaching in, I pulled the plug and water began to pour out through the small hole. It wasn't emptying as fast as I liked, but I needed it to drain off enough so that I could actually tip the thing on its side to pour out the rest. I wasn't sure exactly when I had decided that I was going to paddle across the pond rather than going around, but the more I thought on it, the more sense it made.

I'd crossed a beaver dam exactly twice in my life, and neither time had gone well. The first, I had got my ankle stuck and twisted. The second, I had almost stepped onto a cottonmouth. Had I done so as deep in the woods as I had been then, I'd like as not have died. So going that way was a wash.

Looking the other way, I saw just how long of a walk it would be to get around. The pond wasn't a lake, by any means, but damned if it wasn't long. Those beavers had dammed up the creek, and it had backed the water up for quite a ways. It was long, but fairly narrow, all things considered, so it wouldn't be but the work of a minute to paddle across, I reckoned.

The water had lowered to the point that with a heave, I was able to get the boat up on its side. The rest of the water poured out in a rush, splashing onto my boots. Carefully I lowered it back down, not wanting to have it slam into my shins. Then I slipped the plug back in and shoved her into the water.

I jumped in, walking gingerly so as to not fall out or slip on the algae-slicked bottom. The seat was wet, but I ignored it, taking up the paddle. Its hard plastic was cold and wet to the touch, but I gripped it tight and lowered it into the water.

Then I made my way toward a mock lighthouse of fireflies.

If There's a Bustle in Your Hedgerow, Don't Be Alarmed Now

I was careful to not strike the sides of the boat with the paddle. I had no idea what I might be heading into, so I thought quiet was the order of the day. Thankfully the little bit of a workout that paddling gave me settled my drug-fueled twitches a little, even if it did make my strokes a little uneven at times.

Cutting through the little bit of fog, I watched the tree line as much as possible. The fireflies were still just a-swirling, floating maybe ten, twelve feet above the ground, and as I closed in I gradually became more sure they were circling a small clearing. With dusk falling faster than I had anticipated, though, it was becoming increasingly hard to tell.

The jon boat slipped up onto the muddy bank and I quickly hopped out. With a quick tug, I had the boat pulled up far enough it wouldn't float away on me, and I was left to debate whether or not to carry the paddle with me. In the end I left it in a good, handy spot in the boat. Nothing much around here could be scared off with a paddle, I figured.

I began stalking my way into the forest, making for the string of lights. Keeping my head down, I crouched low enough as I could, while still being able to scuttle around. Not to toot my own horn, but I am no slouch when it comes to sneaky-style scuttling. And the drugs only kinda interfered with that, I think.

A flash of white reached my eyes, and I honed in on that. I was coming up on the clearing, but the edges of it were thick with what looked like rose bushes, which made it hard to see past. But I could see something moving around, and as I focused, my breath skipped.

It was Angie.

I could only see her a little, but I saw enough. She had on some sort of white dress, and as I listened I was pretty sure I could hear her singing. I froze, looking around, sure the King had to be near. I couldn't hear his wheezing, though, nor his laughter. Not even his tears.

As quickly as I dared, I ran up to the row of shrubs. Each was heavily laden with fat blossoms, each a shimmery dark blue in color. The flickering lights that floated a few feet above caused the roses to glisten like swirling waves of the deepest ocean. They drew the eye, but not as much as the woman in the glade.

Angie was walking around a low table, arranging baskets overflowing with cut flowers. Her gown was so white it almost hurt my eyes, thin to the point that it didn't leave a whole lot to the imagination. Her hair was wild, tussled, and tangled, with a few small braids boasting tiny golden rings. But the horns were what stood out most of all.

She wore a leather crown from which curled two ram horns. Each was jet-black, though if that was the natural color or if they had been painted such, I couldn't tell. They looked too dark to be natural. Each curled one full time, encircling her ears, but even though they looked heavy she bore the weight of them easily enough.

I watched a second, amazed to find her actually alive. She looked happy, and healthy, which also surprised me. She was actually *singing*.

Stepping into the clearing, I looked around, just to con-firm again that the King was nowhere to be seen. Raising my hands, I hissed at her. "Angie. Come on, let's get the fuck away from here while he's gone."

She'd jumped as soon as I started talking, giving a little squawk of fright, but her face quickly became sour. "Leave? Why the fuck would I *leave*?" She was making no move to be quiet, I noticed.

I hadn't fully planned for her being alive. I damn sure hadn't planned for her not wanting to leave. "Angie, quit fucking around! We gotta get you out of here, your family is worried sick. Hell, half the county thinks you're dead."

She looked at me aghast. "I am where I want to be. I found Cernunnos—no thanks to you, I might add—and he's taken me as his servant. Why the hell would I give that up for my piece of shit family?"

I gaped. "You idiot," I growled, "that's not Cernunnos. That's a fucking satyr named Evlin. Everyone just calls him the King. He's no more a god than I am." That wasn't entirely true, I thought, but I figured this was no time for semantics. We could debate theology on the van ride home.

A moment of confusion was quickly driven from her face with a dawning realization. "You're jealous! And trying to keep me from my god because of it!" She laughed, a bitter-sounding thing that came from deep in her throat. "I am not giving up being around my god after only a week, that's for damn sure."

I shook my head. "Angie, you've been missing like six months."

The confusion came back, accompanied by a deep flicker of doubt. "What?"

I reached out and snagged her arm, pulling her toward the pond. That was a mistake.

She snatched her arm back with such force that it almost tipped me over. She was little, but damn she was fierce. With a lightning-quick motion she slapped my face. "Get your fucking hands off me!" she shouted.

I was about to start shouting back when my heart stopped.

"Pet?!" came a deep bellow from up the hillside. "What's going on?" It was the King.

A vicious grin came over her face. She ignored my frantic look, and before I could even think about trying to cover her mouth she yelled back, "A man is trying to kidnap me! Help!"

The only thing louder than the sound of the obese satyr crashing through the woods was his thunderous, rage-filled roar.

Gimme Two Steps

There was no time for thought—only time for running. I grabbed Angie, ignoring her shouting and slapping at my arm, and started pulling her in the direction of the boat.

She fought me every step of the way but two things worked in my favor. First, she was a little thing; second, I was a lot stronger than I looked. The drugs had wasted my body to a degree, but what was left was more iron than anything. If I had been a bit bigger myself, I would have just slung her over my shoulder and ran for it.

Rose thorns tore at my clothes, but they were thick enough that I didn't feel too much pain. I could only imagine what it would feel like to be dragged through them in that sheer little number she had on. I might would have felt bad, but then it was her fault we were running from about a ton of fat and pure murder in the first place.

I had a good lead, I thought, but he was moving a lot quicker than I was. I could hear him getting closer and knew there was little chance I was gonna make it to the boat before him. Banking on an elder creature of yore to not be able to swim was one hell of a gamble as well.

Breaking from the tree line, I risked a glance behind me. Angie was there, of course, her face a mask of rage as she struggled against my iron grip. If looks could kill, I'd have been dead a dozen times over.

Behind her, though, I could see the King powering through the brush. As I came into his line of sight, he bellowed, "Marsh!" spit flying from his cherubic lips. He'd be on me in a heartbeat.

With as much strength as I could muster I slung the young woman behind me, slingshotting her around. I let go, which I think sent her tumbling, but I couldn't spare even a split second to look. In one smooth motion I pulled the long-sleeve shirt I had on over my head, leaving my torso bare, the crisp air taking me in its cool embrace.

Each forearm had sprawling, ornate glyphs in yellow paint covering them, glowing faintly in the dusk. The spiral on my chest shown brighter, a lantern in the falling darkness. I braced myself, throwing my left arm up and doing my level best to call on every possible higher power in the history of ever all at once.

The King burst from the trees, lunging straight for me. The stink of him hit me a half second before he did, a stench of soured, rotting fruit and diseased sweat. His hooves churned up pinwheels of muddy soil as he raised a fat fist, driving it toward me. Flabby, pallid flesh struck my arm, then the world exploded.

A burst of light damn near blinded me as he struck my upraised arm. The glyph exploded in a riot of red-gold fire, the paint instantly flaking off in large, hot flakes. My skin blistered red where the paint had been, but I didn't feel it—not at that second, at least. I was too busy being driven back a half dozen feet, sliding back through the mud till my boots were half buried in the ick.

The King had been launched back as well, slamming back into a tree with a sick thud. It was the sound of someone dropping a fat steak on a hardwood floor, only squishier. The tree itself had cracked and was leaning precariously, slowly beginning to fall with a groaning, wrenching noise.

I jumped out of the way, shoving Angie aside with my shoulder as it came down. It fell across the bulbous, sickly form of the satyr, though much to my chagrin it wasn't anywhere near big enough to crush him. The beast was already starting to try and rise to its feet, fighting against the weight of the tree and winning.

One blow—that was all I was able to take. Another and I would be a gooey pile of crushed bones and bloody flesh. The paint was gone from my left arm, the glyph having been spent turning the blow back on the King. If he hadn't hit so hard, it might have been able to take more than the one blow. But then he wouldn't be knocked down where I could maybe do something about him.

Stalking forward, I stretched my right hand, slowly curling the fingers into a tight fist. The King's eyes were rolling madly, his mouth filled with foam, as he raged against the tree. Already he was almost free of it, his fists ripping out huge chunks of the tree and hurling them away.

It'd been a long time since I'd gotten to crow hop somebody. Opportunity wrote large across the skein of my life—I took it. Two quick bounces, then I drove my fist into the corpulent face of the bastard. I jammed as much extra power into the blow as I could pack into that glyph, crying with orgasmic joy as I felt the bones crush under my hand.

I felt the pain of this glyph flaming out. It was made much worse by the extra power I was feeding into it, and the small blisters on my left arm were dwarfed by the deep burns that appeared on my right. Flowing up my arm came a backdraft of deep-purple fire tinged with gold around the edges, like a Mardi Gras parade gone bad wrong.

Staggering back, I looked at the King. His face was a broken, mangled mess but the bastard was still breathing, still struggling a little, even if it was much weaker. One eye was crushed, but the other was locked on me, pure hate flowing from it bad enough to poison any heart with fear. I was spent now, my glyphs gone, and I hadn't even managed to knock the bastard out. Fuck me.

Angie took a step toward him. "Is he . . ."

"Alive, yes. Now get in the fucking boat!" She looked at me, eyes wide with fear. She looked from me to the prone, struggling form of the King and back again. I damn near cried when she struck a trot to the boat. A moment later we were in the water, and I was paddling with all I had.

And I Ra-aa-an

Even over the sounds of my frantic paddling I could still hear the grunts and struggling of the King behind me. I just hoped he stayed out the game long enough for us to get to the far side of the pond. Then we might—*might*—have a chance to make it to the van. If he got up before then, well, I only had one option, and one I damn sure didn't want to take.

The way Angie was looking had me all sorts of concerned. She was staring at me, hard, with a sort of calculating look in her eyes that made me want to squirm. It occurred to me that I had just punched out her "god" and that she might be looking for some sort of replacement. That, or she might be looking to get revenge. A look like that, it could go either way.

The gloaming had its throat slit, and what little light was left was fast bleeding out. It would be full dark soon, only the faint hint of the falling sun coming from behind the trees before me. A flash of light caught my eyes to my left, and glancing toward it I saw the rapid glow of a firefly. Turning my head a bit as I dug the oar into the dark water, I saw the chain of light had broken up, and the lightning bugs had scattered.

"Has it really been six months?" she asked suddenly.

I looked at her. I wasn't quite in the mood just that moment for deep conversations, what with fleeing for my life and all, but I decided it was better to keep her talking and distracted, lest she decide to do something more proactive. "Yeah. Folks been mighty worried about you. Those who didn't just think you was dead, that is."

"So why are you here?" Her eyes were narrow, and even though it was dark, I was pretty sure her knuckles were white from clenching down on the seat.

I'd have shrugged, but that's hard to do mid paddle. "Your daddy hired me to find you. I got a knack for finding lost things."

She seemed sorta surprised by that, enough to stop the questions, at least. I'd got us about three-quarters of the way across the pond and was really getting some speed up. We were gliding atop the water with a quickness, and for a brief moment I allowed myself a nudge of hope. Then I heard a crash behind me and saw Angie's eyes go wide.

Turning my head, I saw that the King had staggered to his feet, having shoved the tree off from atop him. He was wobbling, swaying uneasily from side to side, but taking halting steps in our direction, shaking his head and sending blood drops splattering around.

"Ah, fuck," I muttered.

"Maaaaaarsh!"

I stopped watching him and redoubled my efforts at paddling. There was no reason to think the fat creature couldn't swim, but I was praying that was the case regardless. The shore was getting close, rapidly so, so there was still a chance. I risked one more quick glance back, and my heart fell. The King was trotting now, making his way toward the water, his hooves squelching through the mud.

The boat hit the shore and I started shouting at Angie to get out, even as I was trying to scrabble across the algae-slicked aluminum. She didn't move anywhere near as fast as I would have liked—I damn near ran her over—but she did what I asked.

Standing in the mud, I looked and saw that the King had entered the water and was swimming toward us with long, powerful strokes. He was going faster than you would have thought possible from something so big. There was no way we could make it to the van in time, so now I had a choice: run and hope he would give up the chase, or beg a favor I would regret asking.

I chose the latter, pulling my pocketknife out and flicking out the blade with practiced ease. "You better stand back a bit. Like maybe up in the trees," I said to the woman. It didn't really matter; I just didn't want her distracting me.

Dragging the knife across my palm, I cut a fairly deep gash across my skin. It hurt like a bitch, but less than a punch from the King would, I figured. Holding my hand over the edge of the pond I clenched my hand into a fist, causing the blood to well up faster. It trickled out of my fist into the water below.

Each drop I fed with a little bit of my remaining power, and the crimson pulsed a deep purple before it struck the water. As my blood met the black of the pond, a little puddle of quicksilver formed on the surface before it sank into the shallows. I closed my eyes.

"Uncle Flathead, I have a need," I whispered low enough that Angie wouldn't be able to hear me. Last thing I needed was for her to try and pull a move like this. She'd caused me enough trouble as is, that was for damn sure.

I opened my eyes, staring at the shallows, praying. The King was about halfway to the shore and coming on strong. I tried my best to ignore that, instead focusing on the water, looking and praying. Then I saw a bit of shadow on shadow, and I knew we had company.

The massive, hoary head of a giant catfish slowly broke the surface. Its broad, flat mouth was as wide as I was tall easily, if not more so. A dozen or so whiskers long as my arm sprouted from atop its upper lip, drooping limply as the face broke the surface. Eyes dark as the night sky peered out at me unblinkingly.

Uncle Flathead didn't speak at first, instead taking in a deep breath—smelling me, I guessed. "A Maaarsh," it said in an ancient, deep voice that rumbled like a distant waterfall. "It has been long years since one of your breed has called."

I bowed deeply. It paid to be respectful to river spirits; they had long memories and held grudges that could span many lifetimes. This one had been dealing with my family since before they moved to Jubal County over 170 years ago. Least that's what my grandfather had taught me.

"It has, Uncle. But I have a powerful need." I looked toward the King, who was getting closer with every passing second. "I am being chased and would like time to escape."

The head nodded, then began to sink below the surface. Before it fully submerged, it spoke. "I will call in this favor one day, and you will pay it."

I knew that was the case, and I knew from history that no one ever liked anything Uncle Flathead asked them to do. And that at least one ancestor had died because of it. But between death and owing an old-ass water spirit a favor, I reckoned I would trade sure death today for possible death tomorrow.

The King was only twenty yards away when it happened. The massive catfish struck from below, its mouth open so wide that it could have damn near swallowed the bulbous satyr whole. It hit with enough force that both creatures flew up a dozen feet into the air in a torrent of black water.

Bellowing in rage, the King started hammering its fists into the mouth of Uncle Flathead. The large mouth had the satyr gripped around the waist, and with a splash, they went under. The water became a churning tumult, growing white with froth and tinged with the pink of blood, though whose, who could say.

Turning, I took off running into the woods. Uncle Flathead would keep the King occupied long enough for me to escape, but I had no doubt that both creatures would walk away from their tussle. And if I didn't take the chance given to me, then I would have an even more pissed off satyr to deal with.

So I ran, and thankfully, Angie followed.

AND THE WEEKENDS COME AND GO LIKE TIDES

I slumped into my recliner with a groan. I wished I'd had the foresight to grab a beer from my little fridge before I sat down, but it was too late now; that ship had sailed. So drenched with sweat that my shirt felt like it had been pulled straight from a grimy pool of water, I was too beat to try and tug it off. So instead, I wallowed in my stench and misery and generally just felt sorry for myself.

Yasmine O'Connel had worked me about to death, which I thought wasn't fair at all. I was a hero—not that anyone really knew it—and you just shouldn't work heroes hard. You should shower them with praise, not chores. Yasmine had failed to get the memo, however.

All I wanted was some damn art lessons, and yeah, she'd given me one first thing that morning after she picked me up. Hadn't amounted to a whole lot, but it was a start, I figured. Being wedged in a class with a couple of brats belonging to the girls that worked there was a bit humiliating, which was made even worse when it turned out they was both a damn sight better than me.

After that hour, though, she'd put me to work doing what seemed like every chore that had been put off the last five years. If it hadn't looked like it might storm, causing her to call it a day, I would probably be lying dead in a field, my carcass clinging to an old push mower.

I wanted art lessons, that was for damn sure. Them glyphs of HD's had saved my ass in a big way, and I fully intended to try and take advantage of that. Hell, two days earlier I had even sat there a bit, practicing on one for an hour or two, before I got too high and couldn't focus no more.

I needed art lessons. But damn if it was gonna be worth all this work. I wondered if I could just pay her. My cash reserves were already pretty low again after I went my Jimmy's to stock up, then got caught up on my rent a little bit. But I could probably scrape up a little something.

Supposedly I had a good chunk of money coming, reward money, but I knew how that went. All parties concerned had decided that "amnesia" was gonna be the best way to tackle the whole Angie ordeal. So, officially speaking, she'd just wandered up in her daddy's backyard. So I suspected that big reward offered by Mr. Burdette's job wasn't gonna come through. And I had no doubt he would try to personally make it good. But we all know how well good intentions pay the bills.

All in all, it had me in a bad mood. Unexpected work, getting screwed out of money, almost dying a couple times . . . it hadn't been a great week. In truth, the only good thing, meeting Anna—even that had turned to shit. I hadn't heard a peep out of her since she left my place on Saturday. Above it all, I think that was the biggest bummer. Everything else, that was about par for the course. But my gut told me she was something sorta special, and I'd let her car get smacked around by an angry, fat, naked satyr.

I didn't blame her. It still sucked, though.

It started to rain outside my little shed, and it was a perfect fit for my mood. I was sinking into melancholy, fast, and I had this masochistic urge to steer into the curve instead of fighting it. There was a fifth of Heaven Hill on top of my fridge, which was beside CD player. I could turn up the bottle, then turn up some Type O Negative and just sink into the sordid bliss of depression. Just had to get up out this chair, which I would do just as soon as I got done resting my . . .

A horn honk woke me up. I jumped to my feet, so startled I think I peed a little. My head snatched right, and I saw a little blue Ford Focus sitting in the rain, the wipers just a-swiping. I was so surprised, I found myself standing in the rain a foot away from the door before I even fully realized it. Anna was inside, a smile on her face.

She cracked the window, blanching a bit as a bit of rain splashed in. "Hey there," she started, then her nose crinkled. "Damn, Marsh, smelling kinda ripe there. Guess you've been working or something?"

I laughed and stretched my arms out to either side, doing my best Jesus pose as the rain came pounding down. "Well, just let me stand here a second or two and have a bath. I'll be with you directly."

With a laugh, she rolled up her window and then stepped out into the rain with me.

September Doves

*Being the Fourth Tale in the Redemption of
Howard Marsh.*

HELL OF AN ALARM CLOCK

Monday, September

I woke up to a gun in my face.

To be fair, it was not pointed directly at my face. No, it was just sorta eye level as I lay there on the castoff sofa I called a bed now. That did little to ease my surprise, however. I slowly recoiled toward the back of the sofa, making damn sure to not to make any sudden moves. My eyes drifted upwards as I did, taking in the person attached to the gun.

He was tall—that much was clear—and seemed to be composed mostly of a crisply pressed ink-black suit. He could have walked right out of a black-and-white photograph for all the color he had about him. Even his close-cut hair was about as black as his clothes. And his face was basically just a pair of mirrored shades above a mouth pulled down into a sour frown.

"Marsh," he said by way of greeting, taking a step back away from my erstwhile bed. His voice was familiar, and his tone made it clear exactly how unpleasant he found it to be in my presence.

I tried rubbing the sleep from my eyes. The roll-up door of the storage shed I called my home was wide open, and sunlight was pouring in. "Just come on in and make yourself at home, why don't you?"

"The door was open, Marsh."

In his defense, it could well have been. That would explain why I wasn't woken up by the sound of my heavily dented door squeaking and groaning its way open. I had little memory of last night beyond a few hazy flashes of drugs and booze pouring their way into me, and it wouldn't have been the first time I got too messed up to close my door before crashing.

Looking out, I could see another man leaning against a jet-black suburban. Except for the fact that he looked to be Hispanic, he could have been the armed man's twin. Clearly they had the same tailor. Their vehicle was still running, I noticed.

I sighed. "Guessing Rutherford didn't send y'all on a social call, did he?"

Mr. Pistol shook his head, his face gaining an ever-deepening scowl. "No, he did not. You're going to be coming with us. The boss man wants to see you."

A string of curses flowed through my mind, but I was not awake enough yet to force them past my lips.

The suited man kept talking. "Here is how it's going to go. I am prepared to give you five minutes alone in your shed to get ready if, in return, you keep your damn mouth shut on the ride up to Montgomery. Otherwise, we'll just load you in now."

I remembered this one now. He had given me a ride once before on Rutherford's orders and clearly had decided he wasn't a fan of my brand of smartass. Fair enough—it's been said I am somewhat of an acquired taste. Bribing me into silence with my own drugs, though? I had to admit that was the perfect way to handle me.

Maybe these government boys weren't as hopeless as they seemed. "Alright. Five minutes. Be a dear, would ya, and shut the door behind you as you step out?"

I was already reaching for the little box of oblivion I kept hidden under the ratty recliner that was my only other real piece of furniture.

About an hour later I found myself sitting in a windowless box of a room. The ride up had been uneventful, me mostly keeping quiet, just letting the cocktail of drugs eddy and swirl through my system. The agents had led me inside the bland office building that was the front for whatever the organization actually was, and within moments I was escorted to a dull, gray shithole.

I had been in enough interrogation rooms over the years to know one when I sat inside of one. This particular example was a good bit nicer than what I was used to, however. In the Jubal County sheriff's office, a "new" table would only be twenty or so years old.

The table I found myself sitting at though was nice. No dents, no weird stains, just fine polished metal of some sort. And the chair was fairly comfortable, even if I was handcuffed to it. All in all, I would have felt right at home, except for the discrete drain in the middle of the floor.

That drain had my mind churning in a number of directions, none of which were good. A room in a basement of a fairly nondescript office type building with no windows and only one thick door for an exit was creepy enough. But add a drain into the mix, and I was fairly certain someone had washed some blood down it at some point.

I did not intend for any of my blood to join whatever had been spilled in the past.

The door opened, and two men stepped in. Rutherford, arguably the biggest of many, many thorns in my side, was first. His gray hair was kept cut close, and his clean-shaven face was in its usual frown. He barely glanced at me, instead leaning one black-suited shoulder against the wall as the second man sat down across from me.

While everyone else I had seen was all lean muscle and black suits, the seated man was a bit on the chubby side, and instead of a suit he wore a simple blue polo. He was smiling at me real tentative like, as though I was gonna spring across the desk at him and he wanted to make it real clear he was no kind of threat.

"It's a pleasure to finally meet you, Mr. Marsh. I have followed you—"

"I have places to be," Rutherford said, cutting the tech off. "Brevity is golden."

"Someone's cranky," I said. "You'd almost think you was woke up with a gun in your face and then drug outta bed. Oh no, wait, that was me."

"Marsh, I have no patience today for the usual bullshit games. So shut it, and listen."

The tech had the look of a kid trying to not be noticed while Mommy and Daddy were fighting. When a few seconds passed without me retorting—which, I will admit, was quite an achievement for me—he began to speak.

"A young man caught an anomaly on film and uploaded it to YouTube." The man set a tablet on the table between us, tapping the screen to bring it to life. As he brought up what I assumed would be the video, he carried on talking. "This was filmed not too far outside of Elk Grove, two days ago. It caused enough of a stir to catch the notice of our Boston office—"

Rutherford grunted, causing the tech to flinch. The head agent didn't like me knowing anything about their little agency. Which, if I'm being honest, went both ways. I didn't want to know shit. Knowing shit led to problems.

"Ah, well, here it is." He pressed play as I leaned over to look down at the screen.

The video was jerky at first and out of focus, as if whoever was filming had just pulled their phone out of their pocket. As the screen began to clear I could see trees. They had been standing in a forest, and it certainly had the look of Jubal County. I could see a few half-rusted beer cans laying at the foot of a leaning pecan tree, right in the midst of what looked like poison oak.

A voice was speaking; it sounded like a teenage boy. His voice was cracking pretty bad. Puberty was a right bitch, that's for sure, and from the sounds of things it was doing this boy no real favors. Of course, the terror in his voice was not helping matters at all.

"Y'all don't believe me, watch!" he was saying. He was speaking pretty low, but you could hear him clear enough. "That fucking dog was *right* there!" The camera began to jerk a bit from side to side then as though the boy was looking to get something on screen. And then I saw it.

"Goddamn, that's a big dog," I said. But even as I was saying it, I realized I was wrong.

It looked sure enough like a dog, only huge. I had never seen a wolfhound in the flesh, but I had seen enough pictures. This looked a bit like that, only stockier, like if it had a pit bull for a momma instead. But at the end of the day, a dog, even a really big one, is just a dog.

This one, though, was flickering. You'd see it for a second or two, and then it would just . . . vanish. Just for a split second, and then it would be back. It was slowly stalking its way past that big old pecan tree, headed straight for the boy, just flickering in and out of existence right in front of the camera.

On top of that, its eyes were glowing. For a second I caught myself hoping it was just light reflecting off them somehow, but that pale yellow glow never let up. Even as the thing would flicker, you could see a little echo of that glow bleeding through from wherever it was disappearing to.

"Aw, shit," came the voice from the video, and the camera panned around as the youth took off running. The video became unwatchable, really—just a bunch of scattered images as the boy ran through the woods. He was hollering up a storm now, any thought of talking low gone right out the window.

The video came back into focus as the boy stopped. All I could see was a bit of asphalt, so he must have run back to the road. There was the sound of a car engine coming up the road, but without seeing it I couldn't tell how far off it might have been.

And that's where the video ended.

I leaned back into my chair. "Shit."

"Insightful as ever, Marsh," Rutherford said. "What is it?"

I gave my head a shake. This was a new one on me, for sure. "Hell if I know. Could be a few things, but I ain't ever heard of a Grim or a hellhound flickering like that."

Truth be told, I wanted nothing to do with this. It had a sure 'nuff bad feeling about it. I had a guess though Rutherford had no intention of settling for that, though.

"We have the boy here. You could maybe talk to him," suggested the tech.

I laughed. "I'd just as soon y'all hand me a few bucks as a consulting fee, or however you fine folks file it on your taxes, and then send me on my way. So let's do that."

Rutherford's face split into a grin. That's when I knew I was fucked. The man never smiled unless he had some way to ruin my day.

"Clark, give us a minute," Rutherford said.

Clark glanced toward me, then bobbed his head. "Yes, sir," he said as he scooped up the tablet and rose from the chair. I wouldn't say he scurried from the room, exactly, but let's just say he would not have been out of place with a mouse tail coming out from under that lab coat. It did not inspire a lot of confidence in my current situation.

The gray-haired agent eased himself into the now vacant chair, that wicked smile burrowing right into my very soul. I had to fight to keep my eyes from looking over at that damn drain.

"Let's have a chat."

We Have a Chat

R utherford laced his fingers and set them at the desk. It invoked images of my grade school principal, which made me want to grin. I figured that would just piss the agent off. So, of course, I did it.

The man's eyes narrowed slightly. "It's no secret that I don't like you, Marsh. To me, you are a tool to be used. A tool that I don't mind if it breaks. You have a limited set of uses that honestly could be done by virtually any other . . . *anomaly* the Agency has access to. Ones that aren't barely functioning drug addicts."

"You're too kind," I quipped. "Careful, now, or my ego might just grow legs and run away from me."

"You don't get it. You have this inflated sense of importance without any reason to back it up. You are the guy I call up when I don't want to waste someone good on a bullshit task. Something like this. There is potentially world-ending shit out there, and that is what I send people worth a fuck to go solve. You . . ." His lip curled. "You are who I send to investigate small droughts, and weird dog shit."

I couldn't tell if he was trying to get a rise out of me or just venting his spleen. Either way, I hadn't a fuck to give. You don't grow up with a grandmother like mine and not learn how to shrug off a little emotional abuse. So I yawned.

"This one is actually above your pay grade, since someone might actually be at risk of death. If you didn't have a connection to the case, I would probably let someone actually competent take it on. But it is what it is."

I didn't like the sound of that at all. "Connection?"

Rutherford shook his head. "Clark will fill you in later; that's what we pay him for. But you are going to solve this one. I want there to never be another flickering dog in Jubal County by this time next week. And you will be doing this one pro bono."

"The fuck I will!" I surged forward, forgetting that I was still handcuffed. It hurt my wrist, but worse, made me look dumb in front of the agent, which just made me madder. "You'll damn well pay me."

"No. We won't. Because it is time you learned your place in the world." Rutherford could not have grinned more if he had been a shark. "You have no real concept of the power I have at my disposal. The guns I can bring to bear. With the snap of my fingers I could send you away to prison for a very, very long time, without even a trial. And when I say 'prison,' what I mean would make a CIA black site look like a stay at a beachside resort."

The thought of it chilled me right to the core. I had done time, of course—a good bit over the years. But all county jail type stays. I had a suspicion that if I ever saw the inside of whatever prison Rutherford had in mind, I would never leave it alive. Involuntarily, my eyes darted to the drain.

He noticed. "Exactly. So as much as I would enjoy removing you from my life, I decided I would rather keep you around and make your life miserable on a personal level. So you are going handle this one, for free. And if in a week you can't show me progress, then poof, Marsh disappears. So are we clear?"

My mouth was dry as paper and my throat was tight. I didn't trust my voice, so I just nodded.

He stood, walking toward the door. "Good. One week, Marsh. And don't even try and use the hurricane as an excuse. I'm warning you."

Stepping out, he held the door long enough for Clark and my agent buddy from earlier to walk inside. The agent worked to uncuff me while Clark began speaking. I had to shake my head to jumpstart my brain to working again.

Fear has a way of being a bit distracting when folks are trying to tell you important shit.

"We are going to take you to meet the boy, Hank Durrant, so you can ask him whatever questions you might have." He held up a folder. "I was told you don't email, so I printed out the relevant files for you to look over."

The cuffs came off and I started rubbing my wrists in turn, bringing a little life back into them. "Rutherford said I had a connection to this case. The fuck was he on about?"

Clark handed me the folder and started leading the way out the room and down a hallway, talking all the while. "As you are aware, Jubal County has a higher than average number of anomalies. Well, all of central Alabama, really, but Jubal ranks pretty high on that list. So we funded a digitization of all the county records so we could start cross-referencing them to anything unusual that occurred."

That rang a bell. "I remember that. My aunt works at the courthouse. She bitched for months about all the extra work she had to do."

Clark rolled his eyes. "Scanning documents is not exactly hard work, and we paid for a lot of interns from Troy to help. But anyway, when the video caught our eye, we ran a keyword search against the county documents. A few things cropped up."

The pudgy tech pushed open a door into a small room. A large pane of glass revealed another room similar to the one I'd just been in. There was another table, and around it sat a youth of about fifteen and an older blond man in an expensive suit.

"Turns out there have been a couple other odd deaths in Mr. Durrant's family, including his cousin, Westin Durrant."

"I know that name," I said. It itched in the back of my mind, but I couldn't place it.

Clark smiled gamely. "You probably do. He dated your cousin Krista. She was one of the primary sources in the police file on the young man's suicide. In fact, she was the one who mentioned in the report that he had been complaining about a dog following him in the days preceding his death."

I was a little creeped out by how well this random tech seemed to know my life but decided to leave that be for now. I remembered Westin now, just a little. I had dropped out the year before he died and he had been a grade above me, same as Krista. She had taken it pretty hard, and it was still a little bit of a sore spot between us that I wasn't really there for her. I was already dreading the inevitable guilt trip that would rain down on me when I brought it up to her.

I tapped the folder against my cheek, thoughtfully. "Well, I reckon as soon as the suit is done in there, I have a few questions for the boy."

Clark shook his head. "Oh, you can go on in, that's just his new handler. Working the cover story for that video and all, you know."

I arched an eyebrow. "Just delete it. That'd be easier, right?"

Clark laughed. "On the internet? We delete it, and the conspiracy loons go nuts. But we explain it away by saying it's a young man's attempt at making a new Blair Witch movie, and things die down."

"Are they really loons if this time they're right?"

Clark looked at me, confusion on his face.

"Never mind," I said, walking into the room. Me and the internet were not really on speaking terms. I'm sure it's all well and good, but surprisingly when you live in a storage unit, the cable company isn't exactly beatin' down the door to provide you service.

The suit was mostly composed of a glistening white smile so broad it almost blinded me. I have a thing about teeth—*good* teeth. I could not keep myself from staring, and though I would try and glance over to the boy, I kept coming back to that broad smile.

The Smile stood up and extended a hand. With a voice like honey flowing over silk, he introduced himself. I think I managed to stumble out my name, but all I can be sure of was the perfection of those teeth.

"I will give you two a minute. I need to visit the bathroom anyway," said that smooth, crimson voice, and then my life returned to its usual bleak state.

I gave my head a little shake, then faced the boy. "Hank, right?"

The youth had a face ate up with acne and an unfortunate attempt at a mustache crouching on his upper lip. Behind all that you had the sense that there was a lot of potential, but it was going to take a little work. Nothing time and sense wouldn't fix, though, I supposed.

"Yeah," he said. His voice cracked just like in the video. "You're Marsh, right?"

I nodded. "The agents tell you I was coming?"

"No," he shrugged. "I just seen you around. I think our cousins used to date, back when I was little."

"Yeah, they did. So lemme ask you a few things. That cool?"

He nodded hesitantly. "I guess."

"The thing, the . . ."

"Flicker Dog," he said.

"Flicker Dog? That what you call it?" The name suited. Had a ring to it.

"Yeah," he nodded.

"Alright, well how long you been seeing this Flicker Dog?"

He shrugged a little. "About two weeks, I guess. At first I was seeing it, only I didn't know what it was. Like, out of the corner of my eye I would see it. But, like, every day it gets more clear. It's got so as any time I'm alone long enough, it shows up."

"You smell anything particular when it shows up?" I was hoping he'd say sulfur. Hellhounds were nasty, but I had my ways of handling 'em.

The boy thought for a second. "No, not that I noticed."

Damn. "And you only see it when you're alone? Never when anyone's around?"

"Right. I've been doing pretty good about staying around folks, but sometimes . . ."

I wasn't gonna touch why a teenage boy needed alone time. "Been in any graveyards lately? Say, in the past month?"

"What? No."

Well, there went the riled up Grim theory. Whatever this was, it was new to me. Maybe a ghost? It was a spirit of some sort. I thought about the file in my hand. There might be something in there that would help clue me in.

I couldn't think of another question. "Well, I reckon they got me working to get rid of it. So I wouldn't worry too hard. In spite of what you might hear around here, I'm pretty shit hot."

The boy looked incredulous, but then I don't exactly inspire much confidence in the looks department.

"Thanks, I guess," was all I got in response. Kid could learn a little gratitude, but at his age I'd like as not have cussed me out or something.

Then like a dawn breaking over the ocean horizon, the Smile returned through the doorway. I beat a hasty retreat through the still-open door, muttering goodbyes before I made too much a fool of myself.

Clark and my pet agent were still there, which was good, because a question had come to me all of a sudden. "So Hank is here. His parents know it?"

Clark looked over to the agent. "They do," said my chauffeur.

"They put up a big fuss about it?"

The agent thought for a moment. "The dad had some concerns, it seemed, but his mother seemed indifferent at first. She made the final call to turn the boy over to us, however."

So someone knows at least a little something about what's going on, I thought to myself.

"I reckon I got what I need from here. I'd kindly like to get a jump on things, so I guess run me on back to Elk Grove, Jeeves."

The agent's eyes narrowed. "No bullshit this time."

"Of course not." I winked.

The Widower

As the SUV made its way down County Road 7 I just stared out the window and thought about Krista. She was a couple months older than me, just enough to have had her be in the grade ahead of me. In spite of that, we had been best friends as long as we could remember. Both only kids, we were siblings by default, you could say. When things really went south in the family, we clung to each other to keep afloat.

In a family full of black sheep, you could consider us the blackest, though for very different reasons. For me, it was because of my extracurricular activities, repeated stints in jail, and general snark; for her because despite having more than a little touch of magic, she wanted nothing at all to do with the family except for me. To be fair, I didn't much want contact with the family, either, not even with myself. I was just a bit more stuck than she was.

"See that little barn thing, up on the right? Turn in there." I said, breaking the silence.

The agent, who I had finally learned was Agent Reed, didn't say anything back. He flicked on the turn signal, though, so I at least knew that he heard me. He was ill at me on account of having him take me by my shed first. Reed hated being my chauffeur, so I did all I could to add to his misery.

Asphalt turned to gravel as we pulled into the driveway by the little outbuilding. Before the vehicle was even good and stopped I had the door open, the folder and my travel box of goodies under my arm.

"Well, Reedy, it's a pleasure as always," I said. "Pop by some time, let's have a beer."

"Eat shit, Marsh," he said, refusing to look at me.

I hopped from the car, chuckling all the while. The driveway circled on around back a hundred yards or so to a small trailer. It wasn't new, or particularly nice, but you could tell it was well cared for. There were plants and the like in beds along its front, and you could tell it had been painted at some point in recent memory. For rural Jubal County, that basically made it the Ritz.

Much closer was one of those premade little buildings, storage sheds made to look like cabins or barns. This one looked like a scaled-down replica of an old red barn. In front of it was a white sign with "Kuts by Krista" painted in a blue so dark it may as well have been black.

The agent's SUV was already speeding away back up toward Montgomery before I could even make it to the door. I threw a wave toward Reed, which I twisted around into my favorite middle finger salute. If the man saw, there was no way to tell, so I just went on inside.

The inside was as tidy as the outside, so neat and clean it about made my skin crawl. It was your usual small salon: a few chairs for waiting, a small TV to entertain those waiting, and the larger chair for those who were no longer waiting and were having their hair styled by Krista.

The woman of the hour was sitting in the salon chair watching the TV, which was flipped to the weather channel. She glanced over when I opened the door. "Oh, hey, Marsh," she said, her voice friendly, before going back to her TV watching.

Like all of our clan, Krista was short, barely breaking five feet. But where most of us were black-haired and fairly tan, she was pale skinned with a mess of orange-red curls. She took after our grandmother, whereas I fit in with the rest of the family a bit more.

I set my stuff down on top of a stack of magazines that had been laid out to occupy folks. "Daytime soaps getting too exciting? Made the switch to the weather? They got a paint drying channel?"

She waved a hand at me idly. "Hush. I'm watching about the hurricane."

That stopped me. "You know, you're the second person today to mention a hurricane. What's that all about?"

Krista slowly turned in her chair. "Hurricane Irma?"

I grinned. "You talking about Great Aunt Irma?" She was my grandfather's sister, and a singularly unpleasant woman who still refused to die at the age of 97.

"Fitting, but no." She pointed to the TV. "There's a hurricane coming. It's a category three now but getting stronger. Ringing a bell?"

I let my blank stare answer for me.

"Jesus, Marsh, I get you don't have cable in that shed of yours, but you could pay a little bit of attention to the world at large. It's going to hit in the panhandle is the current prediction. Probably Thursday."

I snorted. "Shit, I thought it might be close or something. Thursday? Hell, it'll prolly hit Texas. You know how weather folks are—they can't get it right two days out half the time."

"If you say so," she replied with a tone that clearly implied nothing of the sort.

"You look busy," I said, glancing around the empty room.

Krista swore. "Granny's got everyone scared off, of course, the bitch. I don't guess you came for a cut? Or, better, actually have money this time?"

I ran my fingers through my hair. It was a little long, a little greasy. "Yeah, I could do with a cut, I reckon. And no cash, but I got some green."

With a sigh she climbed out of the salon chair. "Better than nothing."

Krista would smoke a little weed and do a little drinking, but that was the extent. I knew better than to offer her any of the other goodies in my little box. She would just start fussing, and I'd rather she stay friendly. I pulled a joint out of my stash, then walked over to the chair.

"Damn it, Marsh, when was the last time you bathed? Your hair's greasy as shit."

I thought on it a moment. "Last Monday, I guess. I was over at Lidda's; she let me grab one."

Krista huffed. She had a powerful hate for Lidda, one of my exes. The first big ex, really—an Ex with a capital E, you could say. Truth was, Lidda was ok, long as you knew not to trust her.

"Well if you were over there, you need another bath to wash the skank off you. So let's get you leaned back so I can wash your hair at least. I've half a mind to hose you off out back."

She had my head up under the water in no time. It was a shame no one really ever came by; she was actually pretty damn good at what she did. But that was life. So I just lay there and let her massage the grease and grime right off my head.

By the time she had me washed up, I was ready to get down to business. Soon as I was back sitting up straight, I held my lighter to the tip of my joint and lit up. I let my lungs fill with the smoke, then let it out in barking coughs as I passed it over my shoulder to my cousin.

"You and your skunkweed," she said around the joint. She took a few puffs then passed it back. "Keep it—I'll be too stoned to cut your hair otherwise."

I wasn't one to argue. She started trimming and I smoked that joint down to the roach. I snuffed it out on my boot and put what was left away for safekeeping. I was already starting to feel that green glow I got when I was good and high on weed.

"So, I was up in Montgomery. Compliments of Rutherford."

"That asshole. I wish he'd leave you alone."

"You 'n' me both," I said. "Well, he didn't have me up there for my company. He had some weird shit for me to look at."

"Feel free to leave me out of it," she said. Krista had a powerful but understandable aversion to anything . . . *anomalous*, as Clark might have said.

"You know I usually do. But an old boyfriend of yours came up. The Durrant boy, what jumped from the bridge."

She froze. All things considered, this was better than a sudden movement, I supposed, seeing as she had some rather sharp scissors in her hands.

"Wes? Why?" she said after a moment. Her voice was wary, on edge. I'd have to be careful.

I tried to keep my voice level and calm. "Something you said after. About him having complained about a dog following him around. It came up when they did some sorta records search. On account another weird dog is following around his cousin."

She was slowly starting back moving, the *snick, snick, snick* of the scissors starting back up again. "I don't remember saying . . . wait, which cousin?"

"Hank. He'd have been—"

"I remember Hank. I babysat him a few times with Wes. And you say something is following him? Some sort of family shit?" Her voice was getting a little more heated, and the scissors were going a good bit faster. Nerve-rackingly so. So I would imagine, if I hadn't been so high.

"So it would seem," I replied.

"Well, what are you doing about it?"

I wasn't big on her tone. It was getting a bit demanding, but I let it ride. "I'm here, ain't I? Following up one of my only two leads, so to speak."

"I am not a lead, let's make that real clear," she said sharply. "I barely remember being at the police station, much less what I said there. That was years ago, and I've tried to forget as much as I can. You didn't care, but that was a really traumatic time for me."

I rolled my eyes and was instantly glad she was behind me. "You know good 'n' well I cared. You weren't the only one going through some shit at the time, though."

She loosed a bitter laugh. "Right, your skank—who I constantly warned you about, I might add—got knocked up by someone not you."

I was high, but not high enough to deal with this. "Are we doing this again? Right now? For fuck's sake, let it go. It's been years."

She huffed there in silence for a bit. I knew it was eating at her, but I imagine she was about as tired of the whole argument as I was. It was more reflex than vitriol at this point for both of us.

"So what's your other lead?" she finally asked, breaking the silence.

"I thought you didn't wanna know anything."

"Don't be an ass, Marsh."

I raised my hands, palms out. "Alright. Well, from what I gathered talking to Rutherford's people, I think Hank's momma might know something. I figured I would ride over there, have a chat."

"Ok, we'll ride over there soon as I finish up here."

" 'We'? Whatcha mean we?"

"What, you gonna walk over there? Or you suddenly get a car for the first time in five years?"

The lack of car was a bit of a sore spot, and she knew it. "I had planned on calling up Uncle Hubert Dale to give me a lift."

"Or I could just go with you. Seeing as I actually know the family." She had exchanged her scissors for the buzzing whirr of clippers now.

"You got appointments or something, I'm sure. I'd hate to take you from your work." She jabbed me with the car comment, so I jabbed back with her lack of business. We were best friends but could be righteous assholes to each other sometimes.

The clippers made a sharp whine. "Oops," she said blandly. Her tone made it abundantly clear that it was no accident. "Guess we're just gonna have to go with a buzz cut now."

Fuck me.

The Path, It Just Ain't Clear

I wouldn't dare admit it, but riding with the windows down like we were actually felt really damn good on my scalp. I had ended up making her shave me good and bald after she pulled her little stunt. Not because I particularly cared to be totally bald, but because it was that much more of a hassle for her.

Truth be told, I wouldn't have even minded a buzz cut had that been what she set out to do initially. I'm not much of a slave to fashion, you see. But boy, in the moment, I had gotten a bit hot—scary hot, actually, thanks to the non-green drugs I had in my system. But that passed fairly quickly.

So silence was the order of the day as we barreled along the back roads toward the Durrants. She was feeling guilty, knowing her, and I was keeping quiet so as to make her believe I was still right pissed off. I can be a petty sumbitch when the occasion calls for it.

Krista sighed. "Look, if buy you some smokes, truce?"

We were already under truce, of course—at least in my mind. But I never say no to free smokes. "Yeah. I guess." I turned my head to look out the window, trying to be dramatic. "Still a shit move."

She sighed again. "I said I'm sorry a dozen times now. But you know good and well half the time you ask for a damn buzz cut anyway."

"And each of those times you give me this big, long spiel about how I coulda been a model and such, and why don't I take care of myself better. Yadda yadda."

She reached out and put a hand on my arm. "You really could have. I mean, you're short, but your eyes . . ." She turned me loose. I was mighty self-loathing, but even I had to admit my eyes were something else. A pale blue, like little ice shards. Before life had gotten hard, and when I took better care of myself, I had been quite the looker. Still, even now my eyes could get me into beds I had no business being in. "I wish you'd let me get you help."

"I'll settle for those smokes," I said, cutting off her favorite topic of conversation. "The One Stop is up ahead. Good a place as any."

She nattered on at me, so I did my level best to ignore her. Was my drug usage a problem? Of fucking course. It was killing me, and it was just a matter of time before it finished the job. But it was my problem, and it had its uses. So I let her talk at the side of my head while I chewed on this dog issue. I started flipping through the folder again, though I had spent some time looking at it on the ride from Montgomery.

By the time she had walked back out of the store and handed me my pack of cigarettes, I was no closer to having worked it out. Just not enough information. As she buckled up I started eyeing her over.

We were too young to look as old as we did. Too many bad years, too many bad times—it wears on a person. Sitting close like this, I could see the lines around the corners of her eyes. Worry lines, every last one.

She caught me looking. "What?"

I stared for a few seconds more, making her squirm a little. "You sure you don't remember anything?" I asked at last.

She started the car. She wasn't looking at me any longer, instead focused on getting back onto the road. "I remember too fucking much. Where I was when I got the call, riding in that cop car to the station, the funeral. But no, I don't remember anything about a phantom dog."

I opened the folder up. It had copies of police reports, transcripts of interviews, things of that nature. One of them was an interview with Krista, taken the day after Wes had died. I pulled out the sheets I needed.

"Says here . . . let me find it. The cops had asked if Wes had said anything weird lately. The only thing you could think of was him asking you, and I quote, 'Have you seen any odd-looking dogs wandering around lately? Like a big black stray or something?' He followed that up with 'I think I keep seeing this same weird dog around.' Said all this as y'all were about to watch a movie at his place. Ring any bells?"

A disgruntled look came across her face. It was her thinking face, so I knew she was at least trying to remember. She glanced over. "Is there anything else? I feel like I have a word I can't remember on the tip of my tongue. Like, the memory wants to come, but it's tied up somewhere."

I glanced over the relevant passage again. "Just that he said he kept seeing it most everywhere he went. And that he never told you exactly what made the dog weird."

After a few more seconds she shook her head. "I mean, that sounds right, but I don't really remember it. It's like remembering a remembrance of a memory, if that makes sense."

It didn't, but I let it ride. "Well, that is less than useful."

"What else is in there?"

"Well, there are copies of the files on Wes's death, of course. Besides your bit, Rutherford's folks highlighted a section where one of the cops talked about how he thought Wes had been running from something. That he'd been chased off that old bridge."

"Damn," Krista said, her voice small. "We all knew he wouldn't have killed himself. He was way too happy."

What little I could remember of him, I had thought him pretty well-adjusted. Or as well-adjusted as a young punk kid can be in rural Alabama. "Yeah. Besides that, they have a few other pages in here. About five years before Wes died, he had a cousin get hit by a car."

"I didn't know him, I guess," Krista said.

"Yeah, he was a good bit older than us. Anyway, the driver swore that"—I had to flip to find the name—"Albert ran out into the road as though he was being chased. The guy got tried for manslaughter but walked. Al had a bit of booze in his system, turns out. The only reason they even tried this driver guy was one of the paramedics said that he was raving about a big dog, but by the time the cops arrived, he had shut up about it. They thought he might have been tripping, but all the tests came back negative."

"We should go ask him about it!" Krista said.

I swear. Let someone tag along, and all of a sudden they act like they are in charge. "He's dead. Rutherford already checked. Guy moved up to North Carolina and croaked of a heart attack while banging his wife. Not a bad way to go, really. 'Cept for that whole married part."

Krista grinned. "If I recall, you were engaged once."

"Dodged that bullet, I suppose," I laughed. I'd been engaged twice, though Krista only knew of the once, with Lidda. And I planned to take that second time to the grave, I reckoned. Ah, to be young and dumb again.

"God, yes. If you had married that whore, I'd have never spoke to you again."

"I should have been so lucky," I smirked. "I mean, I'd be on the hook for God knows how much child support, but at least I could ride in silence."

She smacked my arm half-heartedly. "Whatever. You'd be lost without me and you know it. Back on topic, though. Anything else in there?"

"Just a few pictures from that YouTube video the boy shot. Picture of the Flicker Dog." I saw her starting to look toward the folder. "I'll show you when we get stopped. Don't need you wrecking."

"We're about there anyway," she said. "Just down here on the left."

A mile down she clicked on her blinker and turned down a dirt road. It was the kind of red clay road that you knew would turn slicker than owl snot when it rained. But dry as it was, it made for pretty smooth driving compared to most of the dirt roads in the county.

Woods lined the road to our left, but the other side was all cow pastures. I could see a few dozen black and brown cows and one big gray Brahman bull dotting the open spaces. A couple of calves were right by the fence, craning their necks through the fence to chew at the taller grass to be had there.

Krista nodded toward them. "Those are probably Mr. Durrant's. He raised cows back when I was dating Wes. Hank and Wes, their daddies were brothers."

A gap in the woods opened up on our left, and in the middle of it squatted a pair of ratty trailers. A few rusted-out hulks of cars decorated the lawn, such as it was, though there was very little grass and a whole lot of red clay. It had that classy look we poor of Jubal County pulled off so well. Underneath a hideous green beach umbrella, some toothless old woman was shelling peas into a five-gallon bucket. She watched us pass with about as much intelligence in her eyes as the cows.

"Most of the folks on this road are Durrants. Or at least were. This all used to belong to Wes's great grandad, he told me, and over the years they have just split the land up over and over."

"Got a good memory now, seems like," I quipped.

She shrugged, not taking the bait. "It's starting to come back to me. You know, I hadn't thought of Wes in months. There was a time I didn't go a day without crying over him. Funny how things fade."

I let that lie between us. She was right. The human mind is blessedly resilient. Which, when I thought of all the stupid mistakes I had managed to repeat over the years, was as much a blessing as a curse. They say you can't remember what pain feels like. Might be better if we could sometimes.

A green John Deere painted mailbox sat on a white wooden post with FFA carved into the side. Krista turned in by it, pulling up the drive toward a small brick home. The house was clean looking, and the yard had an assortment of those weird concrete yard ornaments you see in roadside shops on occasion. The pasture land went right up to the yard, with only a couple of red painted barns to break up the monotony.

A tall man was stepping out of the closer of the two barns, watching us pull up. He was loading some square bales of hay into the back of a battered Ford, and as we closed in he pulled the trucker hat from his head and ran a handkerchief across his brow. Other than that and the cows, I didn't see any signs of life.

"This is it. And I think that guy coming out of the barn is Hank's dad. So maybe let me make the introductions, since I know these people." She smiled wanly. "You don't always make the best first impressions."

I nodded. I'm not the best of people persons. "When was the last time you saw them?"

"The funeral," she said, getting out of the car.

Sweet Mama, Don't Let Me Down

M r. Durrant was walking toward us. His face was blank at first, maybe a little questioning. As he got close enough to see us proper, he brightened up a bit as Krista gave him a small wave. He returned it with a gloved hand, then proceeded to frown as I came into view.

His skin was tanned a dark brown and as he pulled his gloves off I could see the heavy callouses of a man who had worked hard all his life. He was broad across the shoulders, but the rest of him was wiry and lean. Closing the last few feet, he slipped his gloves into his back pocket and extended his hand toward my cousin. "Hey there, Krista, it's been awhile. You sure have grown right up."

"Thanks, Mr. Durrant, I have a bit," she replied with a laugh.

He nodded and turned to face me. There was no extended hand. "As for you, Marsh, I believe I told you if I caught you on my property again you'd catch a backside full of rock salt from my shotgun."

Seeing as I could not recall ever having been on his property, I was a bit perplexed, to say the least. "Uh . . . what?" was the eloquent response I came up with.

There was real anger in his voice. "Don't think I forgot that time you and your buds came out here cow tippin' and raising all hell."

That certainly sounded like something I would have done. Something I probably still would do, given the right pharmacological inducement. But it just wasn't ringing a bell. This was not my first rodeo, though. "I apologize, Mr. Durrant. I was young and dumb. Well, younger and dumber."

He grunted, making it clear exactly what he thought about that. "You behave yourself, and I suppose we won't have any trouble," he said after a moment. "Now what can I do for you? Hank's gone to visit his uncle, but Dora is in the house somewhere if you're looking for her."

Krista got an awkward look on her face. "Actually, Mr. Durrant, it's Hank we're here about."

A sharp look entered the farmer's eyes, but his face tried to lie and hide it with a smile. "Well, he's at his uncle's. I'll let him know you came by, though, and if you leave your number I'll have him call you."

Krista squirmed. She hadn't expected this, exactly, but I was used to being a bad guy. "We know about Hank. And the dog," I said. "Them agents up in Montgomery sent me. To look into it."

Durrant's face twisted into a snarl. Being caught in a lie rankled him, I was sure, but being caught in a lie by such as me—now that would sting right down to the core. He took a half step toward me, his fist clenched as though he wanted to hit me. At the last second, he caught himself.

"Dora's in the house. I got nothin' to say," he said through clenched teeth. He spun and whipped the gloves from his pocket, jamming his hands into them each in turn.

"Real delicate there, Marsh," Krista said under her breath as she watched the man storm off.

"Maybe we don't pussyfoot around stuff, what say? We didn't need to talk to him no ways; it's the boy's momma we need." I pointed to the house. "She's in there, then let's go."

Krista huffed, but not as hard as she might have. As we walked up the driveway, I noticed a big van with one of those carriers on the back for a motorized scooter. "Dora disabled?"

Krista shook her head. "No, I bet that's for Mrs. Jane. She's Hank and Wes's grandmother. I had heard she wasn't doing well; maybe she's living here now."

We stepped under the carport and Krista knocked on the screen door. A few moments later, a gaunt woman opened it. Her hair was long and black, pulled back in loose braid from which a number of errant hairs darted. She looked tired, heavy bags settled under her eyes. Her brown eyes were suspicious, though, and they flicked toward her receding husband's back.

"Krista. It's been awhile." Her voice wasn't cold, exactly, but it was matter-of-fact, the tone of someone too tired for bullshit.

"It has, Mrs. Dora, too long, really. But that's my fault."

Dora nodded but didn't say anything. An awkward moment passed as she looked over to me. "If *he's* here, I suppose this is about Hank." She sighed, then pushed the door wide. "You better come in."

We stepped in and the smell of cooking peas filled my nostrils. The kitchen we were in was large with a table set in the middle of the room. A deep-blue cloth covered it, a few high-backed chairs placed around it.

Dora though kept walking, taking us into what looked to be a den. The smell of mint filled the air, and I could see hanging from the ceiling fan were a dozen or so car air fresheners. Shaped like little trees, some were a little dusty, while others looked as though they had come fresh from the pack. They swirled on their strings under the slow turn of the fan. Beneath it, though, there was another smell, just a hint. Something the little trees were trying to cover up.

We followed her into a hall, pictures of what must have been young Hank on the walls. A shelf with a few trophies looking to be a mix of baseball and FFA awards, for the most part, was to the left, and to be honest those were far more interesting than the fading pictures on the wall.

Dora stopped in front of a closed door. "She likes it to be dark, says light hurts her eyes these days. But she's who you need to talk to." She opened the door. "Momma Jane, I have a couple guests for you. Couple of Marsh children."

"Oh . . . ok," came a frail female voice from within. "Thought they might sooner or later. Let them in."

The smell came to me now. It was the smell of sickness. That antiseptic smell of strong cleaners trying to cover the smell of piss and just not quite doing the job. As I stepped into the darkened room the smell only got stronger, joined by the subtle hiss of a breathing machine.

I looked over to Krista, a tickle at the back of my brain. "Maybe you could talk to Mrs. Dora a bit. I got this." I glanced toward the older woman. She just shrugged.

Krista looked toward the dark room. "Ok, sure."

Dora closed the door behind me, and I about let out a little squeak of fright. The room was dark as night with only the tiniest sliver of light coming from a minute crack in the blackout curtains. It cast a little line of light across my foot, providing just enough light to hint at the contents of the room.

A bed took up most of it, and I got the sense of a dresser to my right. The rustling of bedding hinted at movement I couldn't see within the depths of the room, which only amped the creep factor up to eleven. I was twitchy as all hell and about ready to just run for it. I couldn't stand being around sick folks, and I'd had too many bad experiences in the dark.

"Sorry about the dark. My eyes . . . I get migraines." The woman's voice was thin and reedy, hardly much more than a whisper. "If . . . this is about Hank, isn't it?"

I nodded, then remembered the darkness. "Yes, ma'am. Some government folks are having me look into it. Try and save him."

Jane sighed, I think. She sounded so weak, she could have just been trying to catch her breath. "I don't think he can be. Saved, I mean."

She might well be right, I knew. "Well, maybe let me be the judge of that. I'm somewhat of an expert, you might say."

"Your granny's the expert. But I'll tell you what I can."

She paused a moment, gathering up her thoughts, I guessed. When she spoke, her voice was a little stronger than it had been. "Twenty odd years ago, I was lying in bed. I was alone; Earl, my husband, he had died the year before. I could still get around pretty good then, you see. I wasn't stuck in bed like I am now.

"It was close to midnight, I suppose, and I had been asleep but something woke me up. I wasn't sure what at first, but then I noticed this yellow glow. It was real faint at first, but I sat up and took to staring at it. As I watched that glow . . . it took shape into two big eyes. And then all a sudden they was on the face of this huge dog. Like it just poofed into my room.

"I was so scared I couldn't even scream. I was trying, but nothing would come out. Then that dog, it started coming toward me. It was so big, it didn't have no problem stepping up onto the foot of my bed. It stopped there a minute, just staring at me. Its body would flick away for a second, then right back, but those eyes, they stayed the whole time.

"It pulled the rest of itself up on the bed. It was so close I could feel it breathing on me. I wanted to run, but my body, it was froze solid with fear. It put a paw on my chest and pushed me down onto the bed. I knew I was done for. I could feel its weight pushing down on me, and I started sinking down into the bed.

"It put its face down right in front of mine, those eyes drilling holes into me. I could feel a heat coming off them, like standing by a fire. 'Soon,' it said. And then it was gone.

"A month later, my grandson Tommy wrecked his car. Hit a tree and burnt up."

Her breath shuddered. "Five years later, that dog came back. And a month later Albert got hit and killed. And five years after that, Westin killed himself. And now Hank . . ."

She had started to cry. I felt like I should reach out for her, give her a pat or something. But that room had me all twisted, and the story she was telling wasn't helping.

"Each time that dog comes, one of my grandbabies dies," she choked out around her tears. "When it came for Westin, I went and saw your Granny. I knew her from way back, and I begged her to help. She said she would see, but Westin still died. He still died! And now it's come for Hank! Please, you got to do something!"

The old woman was about as close to shouting as someone with all but dead lungs could muster. My eyes had adjusted to the light enough that I could see the outline of the sickly woman. She was skeletally thin from what I could see, as though the life was being leeched right out of her. She couldn't have much longer; no one could be that thin and live for long.

I thought of asking her to calm down, but from my experience, telling a woman to calm down typically ends poorly for me. "Mrs. Jane, Hank is safe. And I'll put an end to all this, never you mind. Alright?"

"That's what your granny said," she sobbed.

"Well luckily for us both, I ain't her. I keep my word, unless I can't. I aim to put a stop to this, and I will." That was mostly true, even. She must have taken me at my word, because her crying eased a bit. It didn't stop, but it wasn't the wracking cries of a moment ago I had been afraid would break her thin frame in half.

I didn't have the heart to tell her that one way or another she would be dead inside a week—two, at best, no matter what I did. "It's all gonna be ok," I lied.

Imagine What Tomorrow Brings

"So what's going on?" Krista asked. She had bummed one of my cigarettes and had to speak over the sound of the cracked windows.

I sighed. "Krista, I don't think you really want in on this. I appreciate the ride, and the introduction and all. I do. I appreciate the shitty haircut and the smokes. So take my boundless appreciation, and my advice, and leave it be."

"So what's going on?" she repeated, doing that thing where she pretended not to hear me.

I just rolled my eyes. "Fine, then. It's a curse. Jane back there pissed somebody off royally about twenty years ago. Whoever it was knows a good bit more than me but isn't quite on the level of Granny—least they weren't at the time. So it's slowly killing Jane by sucking the life from her to fuel a curse that kills off her grandsons. Nasty, nasty shit. If whoever cast it had been a bit more powerful, it likely would have run its course in about a year. Regardless of how this plays out, Hank will be the last one affected. Cause ol' Jane there will succumb to the curse finally in a week or two."

Krista looked suitably horrified. "Jesus, that's horrible! So did you break it?"

"Nope," I said as I shook my head. "That juju's too big for me. And even if I did, Jane's too far gone. She would just suffer longer."

"There's gotta be something you can do."

I squirmed a bit. I didn't like admitting I didn't have the ability to do something. "I don't really know. Maybe if she dies before the curse kills Hank, it'll go away and he'll be safe. But then maybe if she dies before it kills him, the power of her death will just strike him dead with a heart attack on the spot. The thing to do would be to have the person who cast it lift it."

"Well, who cast it? Let's go find them and make them."

I turned my head and just stared at her a moment, that sort of blank stare you give folks who are saying stupid shit. "First, I haven't the fucking foggiest who cast it, and she couldn't remember anyone she had pissed off bad enough for such as this. Second, twenty years ago, whoever did this already had more skill and power than me. What the fuck makes you think I can 'make' them do anything they don't want to do?"

She opened her mouth, then closed it. She repeated this process a few times before I finally just said what she couldn't.

"You're thinking I should go hit up Granny, see what she knows. See if she can break it." Krista had a powerful, justified hate of our grandmother, and the thought of going to her for help was anathema to everything she believed in.

My cousin gave a little regretful nod. "Yeah, basically."

I hadn't shared the snippet that Granny had already gotten called on this case. There were some dark implications there that I needed to explore before I shared that with Krista, if I ever did. "Go with me on this one, but she's out of the picture for right now. For reasons."

She flicked the cigarette out the window and gave a little sigh of relief. Despite what you might think, Krista was actually the old witch's favorite. That was actually the source of most of their hate, in fact. So I knew it was a relief to Krista to not be bringing Granny in. "Then where are we? Where do we go from here?"

"To my shed."

"Huh?" she asked, rolling up her window.

I gestured off in the general direction of Elk Grove. "Take me home. To my shed. That's where we go."

"And then what?"

"I know you're expecting a big break in the case or some shit. But we've more or less hit a dead end. I got some angles I can maybe work tomorrow, but that's tomorrow. Tonight, drugs and, depending on what drugs, either sleep or more drugs. All depends on how I'm feeling."

I was feelin' low, so it turned out to be a handful of downers, and then sleep.

You Float Through Your Life as a Ghost

I t was near noon when I peeled my head off the pillow. My cheek was fairly stuck to it with a puddle of drool, as per the usual when I went on a deep dive with pills. I was still groggy and thickheaded, but the pressing need to empty my bladder drove me from the comfort of my sofa. Honestly, it was always a blessing when I woke up after hittin' the pills. I knew it was just a matter of time before the day came that I didn't wake up. It would have been a sobering thought if it wasn't for the fact that it was less a revelation than a constant fact of life.

I was pretty proud of my new furniture, though. It was actually a foldout couch, one I could turn into an actual bed. I didn't do it most nights, as it was sorta a bitch to unfold and then put back. And when it was unfurled it took up damn near every inch of floor space I had, requiring that

I shift my recliner around. But on the weekends, when Anna was staying over, it worked out right nice.

It would have been nice to wake up next to her, but she was a stickler: During the week she worked and went to school and I wasn't to bother her. I was her little weekend boy toy, and I was ok with that. It had just been a long time since I'd had a girlfriend I actually wanted to spend time around on the regular. At least, I was pretty sure she was my girlfriend; I hadn't asked yet. Seemed like a good way to fuck things up.

By the time I took a leak, got dressed, and got good and flowing with my drugs, HD was pulling up in his van. He'd already been on the way when I texted, so I didn't have to wait much, which was nice. Feeling generous, I shared a fat joint with him that we smoked as I got him caught up on my current situation. He was good about not interrupting, so I was able to get it all out by the time I started to tuck away the couch.

"Sounds like quite a mess you got there, son," he said when I finished.

"In-fucking-sightful. Got anything to add? Like an idea of who or what might be behind all this?"

He gave a noncommittal shrug. "Not exactly, no. Though I got some ideas, maybe."

"Well, anything you got, I need. 'Cause I am dead in the water otherwise, and I don't much fancy going to fuck-me-disappearing-forever prison."

"I reckon you're right about it not being a grim, or a hellhound. I think it's a Cu Sith."

The words sounded like "coo shee" the way he said it. I'd heard the words before, I was pretty sure. There was an echo of a memory there from when I was really little, something my Granddaddy had told me, I think.

"Big dog spirit that's a warning of death and carries your soul off to the afterlife when it's done."

"It doesn't do the killing?" I asked.

"I mean, I ain't no expert, but I don't think so. Not unless you just up and die of fright. None of the stories Dad ever told me had the Cu Sith doing the killing, at least." He lit a cigarette as he talked. "I think the Flicker dog, it's more of a side effect than anything. Someone done up a wicked bad curse, and the Cu Sith is more of an omen than an active participant."

I frowned deep as a thought struck me. "So the curse kills these kids, not the dog. Least not directly. Basically, bad luck kills them. So, in theory, the dog ain't even got to be there?"

HD looked at me. "Maybe? Not exactly like there is a hard science to this or anything. All I got are guesses. Why?"

"Currently, they are not leaving that Durrant boy alone on the thought that the dog won't come around if there is someone there, and if the dog don't come around then he'll be ok. But if the dog ain't actually doing the killing . . ."

"Then he could die at most any moment," HD finished my train of thought.

"He dies, you can bet your ass Rutherford is going to fuck me." My stomach sank. "Hell, for all we know they are on the way right now to haul me off to jail."

"You said the old lady looked like she had another week or so in her? Then that's doubtful. You should have at least that long. I figure that curse will suck the last of the life from her to finish him off. But that is a bit of a ticking time bomb."

I found myself chewing on the side of my nail without realizing it. It'd been a bad habit when I was younger, but most of my other bad habits had replaced it. Nail chewing showed just how worked up I was getting, which in turn got me even more worked up.

The next hour wasn't pretty. It weren't HD's first rodeo when it came to talking me down from a precipice, but regardless, it ain't ever a romp in the park. Drug-fueled paranoia doesn't make you the most rational of sorts, and to be fair, even without the drugs I had my moments of impulsive irrationality. This little tornado of terror involved a lot of shouting, not a few tears, and more than a little cowering in the corner.

He's a pretty good sport about it all and only had to choke me out once. When I got my breathing back, it was a little easier to start taking those deep breaths he was prattling on about, which started the downward spiral on the path of leveling off. He was a short, wiry little shit, same as me, but damn if he didn't have some strength in those arms of his.

"We good now?" he asked for the third time. I replied in the affirmative, and this time it actually seemed to take. My thumbs kept flicking a bit, as if they wanted to jump up and pop their nails into my mouth once more, but I tucked them into my fists and clenched down hard till the urge passed.

"First step, you need to go back and talk to that old lady again. No one gets a curse like this laid on them for no reason. I'll run you over, so don't worry about that. Maybe help work something loose. Sound good?"

I looked down at my clenched fists. "I reckon."

Round and Round

We bumped down the red clay road toward the Durrant household just as Krista and I had the day before. It felt a little weird to be coming back so soon, sort of like I was reliving a major failure, in a way. Like if I had done a better job my first time, then this trip wouldn't be needed. I was still all out of sorts after my breakdown earlier, and I felt drained on top of everything else. I needed to get into my drugs, try and even myself out, but I was afraid to do so right before meeting with the old lady.

And let's be real: I had a real desire to get into those drugs. But *need*? Oof. They were just as likely to fuck me up as even me out.

We rolled past the little collection of ratty trailers. The old woman was still sitting there, still shelling peas. The only difference was now she'd been joined by what looked to be a daughter who was about as broad as she was squat, wearing a pair of shorts designed for a much narrower expanse of flesh. We had the poor luck to be driving by as the woman was bent over picking up another bucket. Magic is real, because those shorts didn't split wide open.

Compared to the Durrants I had met, this lot were some sorry specimens. Not as bad as me, maybe, but no peaches, that was for sure. "You know any of these folks?"

HD glanced over at the slum. "Oh, yeah. Everyone on this road, pretty much, I think. I went to school with a few of the Durrants back in the day. Ain't my first trip out this way."

"Oof," was all I could muster.

He shrugged and glanced my way. "Every family got its black sheep."

I let that slide over me. I knew damn well what an outcast I was; I didn't need the constant reminders. And to be honest, my family was sort of shitty all around, least from where I stood. It was no great loss to be on the outside looking in most times.

We rolled into the driveway as I had before and climbed out. Unlike last time, however, Mr. Durrant must have been out in the pasture or in the house, as he didn't come strolling up to say hello. Instead Mrs. Dora stepped out the side door, wiping her hands with a towel. She stood there expectantly as we walked up.

"Dale, been awhile. And Marsh, back again, I see."

"Yes, ma'am," my uncle said, leaning in to give the woman a hug. Dora hugged him back, but I could tell it seemed forced. The way she glanced back over her shoulder told me all I needed to know about how it had gone down between her and hubby after we left.

The older woman clutched the towel between her hands, twisting it. "If you've come to see Momma, you'll have to come some other time. She's resting."

She was lying.

HD frowned, and glanced over to me, embarrassed. "Oh, we're sorry. Is there a better time we might could call?"

"I think you've bothered her, and us, enough, don't you think?" She looked dead at me for the first time. They weren't kind eyes. "My husband would have a pure fit to know you was back."

I just stared back. I didn't have time for this. "Mrs. Durrant, I'm gonna be rude for a second. Not addressing all this isn't an option. As I see it, there ain't but two choices. Either someone talks to us now, or someone talks to us later this afternoon, or this evening, or around midnight, or one of the many, many times I am prepared to have Krista or Hubert Dale drive me over here."

"Howard," HD said softly, which annoyed me. He knew what was at stake here.

I ignored him, just continuing to stare into Dora's eyes. "You may have forgot your son's life is at stake here, but so is mine, and I damn sure ain't forgot. So, what's it gonna be?"

For a moment I felt bad for the woman. She was under a world of stress. Dying mother-in-law, cursed son and all that—it was a heavy load to carry. But what kept crossing my mind was the mental image of a drain in an interview room floor.

"Momma is resting," Mrs. Durrant said after a moment, chewing her bottom lip. "I mean, she's not asleep, but she is tired. Could I help, maybe? I'd rather she was left alone."

I decided I would give her a chance, give her a small victory. "Twenty years ago, something happened that pissed somebody off. At your mother-in-law. Anything stand out?"

"Momma? She'd never hurt a fly . . ." Dora's brow scrunched up. "We'd been married a couple years at that point, but we'd dated a good while before that, and I can't think of anyone being mad at her. Only thing I can remember is Granddaddy Wilford dying. That would be my grandfather-in-law. He died around then."

"Twenty years ago?" I checked.

"More like twenty-two or three now, I guess, is when he died. It was right after we got married, I think. I remember the funeral pretty well; it was rainy." Dora sighed. "Momma was all kinds of upset, mostly 'cause Aunt Delva wasn't there."

"Delva?" HD cut in. "She lives up the road, right?"

Dora frowned and nodded. "Her and her brood. She was still run off with her last boyfriend at that point." Dora leaned close, lowering her voice. "He was Black. She missed the funeral 'cause they were still off up north somewhere."

That's the thing about the South. The racism is never far away.

"You can't think of anything, anything at all? No reason for anyone to be mad at her? And I mean *bad* angry?"

Dora shook her head, looking sad. "Everyone loves her. Even when her bitch of a sister Delva came back after leaving that hoodlum, she was nice enough to let her have a little land to live on. Woman's as close to a saint as I've ever met, I suppose."

"There has to be something, Dora," HD pressed. "Someone's cursed your family, and no one does that for no reason."

The woman looked almost frantic. "I don't know! Every-one gets along most ways, other than the occasional little squabble, but that's all families! Aunt Delva is the only sour grape, but she keeps to herself—always has."

"Dora!" came a yell from near the fence line. Her husband was standing there, glaring at us with a rage-filled face.

"You need to leave," she said, turning back to us. "Leave, and don't come back. Please. We're simple people, and we just want to be left alone."

I shook my head at her but turned and stalked back to the van, not saying another word. Well, I did let my middle finger express my hello to Mr. Durrant. I knew it wasn't totally their fault; most folks, they subconsciously fight back so as not to understand how the world really works, the things that go bump in the night. It made a lot of folks real difficult to talk to at times. But these people, their son was going to die, and they were being angry little shits. If my life hadn't been on the line as well, I'd have left them to rot.

HD slouched behind the wheel. "That went well," he mut-tered, putting the van in reverse.

"Fucking people, man," I swore. "Not like people's lives are on the line or anything."

"Hey now, they're a couple of scared parents. Can't fully blame them, especially when their only salvation seems to be a drug addict with your kinda reputation. Doesn't exactly engender a lot of confidence." He straightened out the van, leading us back up the dirt road. "Besides, I got a little bit of an idea from it, at least, though you ain't gonna like it."

My eyes narrowed. "What?"

"Tomorrow, you walk down to the courthouse and go see your Aunt Crystal."

My narrowed eyes scrunched closed. "Fuck me."

"Look, you know good as me any sort of gossip always winds up in her ear. She probably knows things about that family that Dora don't. And since you can't get in to see Jane, this is your best bet to find out why someone got this curse spelled up."

That stopped me. "You think someone got this curse made for them, not that they did it themselves?"

HD shook his head. "What you got here is a damn mess. Curse this nasty, it had to be spelled up by someone with some real knowhow. The kind of person that would know how to cast it and have it be over and done with quick like, not over twenty damn years. They spelled it up, and then gave it to whoever actually cast it. Someone who didn't have any real power themselves. That's why it's taking so damn long."

I started. That made a lot of sense, actually. I had no idea myself how to "give" someone a spell, but I knew it was possible. Granny was known for her spell jars; it's what kept her in business. "Do you think—"

"Your Granny? No, I don't think so."

Frowning, I disagreed. "I mean, she got called in and said she'd look into it and then didn't do shit about it. Sounds like she had a hand in it to me."

"Right enough. But I think if she'd done it, she wouldn't have ever agreed to even see Jane, much less agree to look into it. Also—and I know you don't have a real good opinion of your Granny, but she ain't a really killer. This is nasty shit."

I snorted. HD knew what a demon Granny was, but he also had a blind spot for her as her baby boy. I, on the other hand, had zero doubt that if someone got between Granny and what she wanted, they would wind up dead if that's what it took. The whole county wasn't scared of her for shits and giggles. There was real fear there, and I had seen at least part of the reason why. I knew better. "If not her, then, who? 'Cause I can't think of anyone in the county with even a whiff of power that would pull some shit like this."

HD nodded. "You're right. Only I don't think they are in the county, least not for the past fifteen, sixteen years or so. I think Morgan did it."

"Who the fuck is Morgan?"

"You don't remember Aunt Morgan?" He seemed gen-uinely surprised by that. "Morgan, or Aunt Mogan as you called her when you was real little, was learnin' from your Granny. This was before all the shit with Grandpa, and then Krista. She was nice enough, and God, was she beautiful."

"You saying I have a hot aunt? How very Alabama of you, Uncle," I said.

"She wasn't actually your aunt. She's no kin of ours, and that was the problem, really. She wasn't anyone's kin. She was a briar witch."

"Oh . . . oh, fuck. Well, that makes sense."

A Debate Over the Distribution of Beers

H D had the decency to feed me an early supper from McDonalds, and he even slipped me a five when he dropped me off back at my shed. I did my best to ignore his preachifying in my direction, but cash always had a way of procuring my attention. When you have a reputation such as mine, gainful employment is often not the easiest thing to be had, and this Rutherford bullshit was fucking with those few avenues I did have. So if listening to him tell me that I was gonna wind up dead from all the drugs I took netted me a fiver, well, that would be the easiest money I earned all month.

It was closer to six than five when I got out of his van and watched him pull away. Too late in the day to really start anything proper, but early enough to make you think you might oughta try. With a grunt, I rolled up my shed door and stepped inside. I decided the first order of business was to take stock.

I knew, in a general sense, that a curse was causing the Flicker Dog. I had even probably figured out who spelled up that curse thanks to HD. I still had no idea why, but maybe Aunt Crystal would be able to help me with that tomorrow. I figure that out, have them break the curse, and boom goes the dynamite. Back to business as usual.

With the five he had just given me, I had a total of about five dollars and some loose change to my name. Rent was due on the shed in about a week. Well, rent for this month, that is. Rent for last month had been due for about three weeks. So my financials were less than ideal, but to be fair, they were slightly better than normal.

I also had an almost full box of oblivion. I had enough drugs and goodies tucked away in there to keep me occupied for days on end, certainly enough in cash value to pay off several months' rent on the shed, but a man has to have priorities. Ralph Mason was too scared of me to even try to evict me until I was at least three months behind.

All this added up to one thing: I would walk over to the Dairy Queen, get some ice cream, come back, and get fucked up on a truly epic level in hopes that something in my mind would shake loose. And if it didn't, at least I would be high enough to deal with living in this shit town.

Money burning a hole in my pocket, I sat up from my recliner and began making for the DQ. It shared a fence with the U-Store-It, so it wasn't exactly a long trek. A few bays down, the door to Corey Davis's shed was open, and I gave a little wave as I passed by. The little accountant, kicked out by his wife some time back, was eating a TV dinner while trying to watch some show on his battered set. It may come as a shock, but living in a shed doesn't make for great reception. The man nodded back, then went back to trying to fiddle with the antenna while not spilling his food.

A few minutes later I was back, cookies and cream Blizzard in my hand. My teeth—what ones are left—were all kinds of sensitive, and all that cold was a literal pain to eat. But I had a sweet tooth, and most times I just couldn't give me no for an answer. So with a spoon full of brain-freezing goodness, I leaned back into Corey's shed.

"Corey, why would you want to kill an old lady and her grandkids?"

The round little accountant was more than used to my oddness at this point and was still struggling with the antenna, so his answer was distracted. "Folks only kill for money or love, Marsh. *Law and Order* taught me that."

I left him to his struggles and spent the next ten minutes alternating wincing in pain and basking in sugary pleasure. I thought about what he said, figuring there had to be some truth to it. Whoever was behind that curse, money or love would be somewhere to be found, I bet. My guess was love. Folks after money don't tend to have the patience to play the long game.

That at least gave me a little something to go on, something I could ask Crystal about, much as I hated to talk to her. Maybe I could maybe go hit up old lady Jane again, ask her some questions about her love life twenty years earlier. That would no doubt be a blast of a conversation, assuming her children would even let me in again, which seemed real unlikely.

I was only barely settled in and hadn't even gotten into my choicer selections from my box of oblivion when Krista pulled up. That was annoying, as with her there I would have to settle for just some weed—at least until she drove off. And if I was being honest, I was getting sorta peopled out. It felt like I hadn't had much of a moment to myself really in far too long.

"Cracked the case yet, McDuff?" she asked as she stepped inside. The little orange bulb was on, bathing us both in a dingy glow, making her face look harder than I think she was aware of. She was trying to act cool, but there was an edge to her. Not that anyone else would probably have noticed, but I did. I also noticed the six pack of High Life in her hand.

"How 'bout you toss me one of those and we discuss it?" I said with a wink. She pulled off one from the plastic rings and handed me the rest to put in my fridge. There was just enough room to hold them once I had pulled myself one free of the plastic.

"Three of those are mine, so don't get greedy."

I drank a good bit faster than her, so I had my doubts she was gonna get all of her half of the sixer. I suspect she knew that as well and was just putting up a fuss to make a point. Least, that's how I decided to preemptively justify drinking more than my fair share of her beer.

She started telling me about her day, which was exactly as boring as I would have predicted if I'd been asked ahead of time. It was the sort of inane small talk that I hated, and the kind I didn't rightly expect from her. She was one of my favorite people precisely because she hadn't made a habit of wasting my time like this. But I had a suspicion she was working her way up to something, so I let it ride and drank her beer with only a light dusting of sarcastic comments.

As she cracked open her second beer, she finally got down to it. She was camped out on my couch, across from where I sat in my recliner, her legs folded under her Indian style. Flicking a strand of hair out of her eyes, she started. "So, you getting anywhere with Hank?"

I snorted at the way she said it. She was trying so hard to sound disinterested, like it was only a passing thought and not the whole damn reason she'd come out to visit. It'd probably been eating at her all day, sitting in that salon of hers with nothing to do but watch the weather channel and think about shit she knew she ought not be thinking about. Stuff she'd shied away from for years now. But once you open that door, even just a crack, it starts to pour in.

Grinning like a possum eating briars, I proceeded to tell her what all had transpired since yesterday. Of course, it wasn't a whole lot, but it was enough that it made it seemed like I was really on the verge of getting some-where. Which, hell, I might have even been, all things considered. But that was when Krista's launched her first surprise of the evening.

"I remember Morgan," she said when I finished. "I'm kinda surprised you don't, actually. She really liked you. A lot more than she liked me, that's for sure."

I frowned. I was drawing a hard blank on the woman in spite of what everyone seemed to think I should remem-ber. But my memories of being a kid were like that, all full of gaps and holes that had only gotten wider and deeper with years of drug use.

"HD said she was a briar witch. She start going crazy and leave?" I asked.

There were two kinds of folks what could use magic. Those who got it from their family, generation on generation of use, the elders training the children on down through the centuries. Folks like the Marsh clan. And that training and exposure over the long years kept the magic from driving us crazy.

The other kind, they were folks with no history of it in their blood. That came into the magic on their own, without any sort of built-up, innate tolerance. And given enough time, the magic would drive them crazy. Sometimes just a little, sometimes a lot. Almost always dangerously in some way—least that's what the stories said. There were lots of different names for them, but here in the Deep South, we'd just always called them briar witches.

Krista shook her head. "No. Granny ran her off when she realized how jealous Morgan was getting over the training I was starting to get. It was not long after they realized how strong . . . it . . . was in me."

It was shaping up to be quite the week of broaching shit we tried to not talk about. Her training was a particularly sore subject between us. She had knowledge locked up in that stubborn head of hers that I would have killed to get. Learned at the feet of Granny, which, while I didn't envy her the time spent with that old bitch, I did want to know what she knew so bad that I could damn near taste it.

But I'd had the poor luck to be born male and then have my grandfather, my teacher, die before I could learn anywhere near enough. Granny used me well enough, but teaching me? Never.

And most galling of all, Krista never used her magic. She'd turned her back on it, hard, and acted like she'd never had it to begin with. It made me mad enough to spit when I thought about it, so I generally just didn't think about it. And usually Krista kept herself from reminding me.

"So when you became Granny's pet, this Morgan woman got run off. Sounds about right." I tried not to say it real mean, but I could only do so much.

"I'm not her pet," Krista spat. She sucked her teeth, taking a breath. She was trying to calm herself down, and I decided to let her. I wanted to see where she was headed with all this, and if I got her too riled up she'd keep her mouth shut out of spite. It was a family trait.

We sat there in silence for a time. I let my focus shift to the third beer I was cracking open. I was working hard on pounding them down, and the faint flicker of what might become a buzz was flitting around the edge of my brain. I just needed to cram a few more beers in with a quickness and then I'd be in business. Luckily, Krista was so lost up in herself she didn't seem to be aware of how fast I was sipping.

So I was surprised when I glanced over and saw that she was crying. She was being real quiet with it, not even sniffing and snuffling. There was just a faint glistening of wetness on her cheeks where a few tears were rolling down. She wasn't even wiping at them, no doubt trying to not draw attention to the fact.

"Do you . . ." Her voice was thick, and she swallowed hard. There was some real emotion there, a tight knot of feeling that she was trying to keep buried down deep. She took a deep breath, the kind of shuddering type folks loosed when they were fighting to keep it together. "Do you think I could have done something? Back when this happened to Wes?"

My eyes widened a bit. I hadn't even considered that. By the time Westin and her had hooked up, Granny had given up trying to give Krista any more lessons. She'd made it clear just how little she intended to have magic be a part of her life, and Granny had settled into the current cold war of trying to put enough indirect pressure on Krista that she'd eventually buckle and come crawling back to be her perfect little heir.

But just 'cause she didn't use it didn't mean she didn't know things. Maybe she knew something that could have broken the curse, something I'd never been taught. For a second I got a hint of just how guilty she must have been feeling now, and my heart broke for her. We fought like cats and dogs, but I did love her like the sister I'd never had.

So was there something she could have done? Maybe. Granny was a good curse breaker, it was said, and I had no reason to doubt she'd taught a bit of that to her heir apparent. So probably. "No, I don't think so," I said softly. "You didn't have any sort of clue it was a curse, so what could you have done?"

She sniffed. "But maybe if I hadn't tied to ignore things so hard, I would have picked up on the clues . . ."

"Krista." She looked over at me. I just shook my head. "No."

Then the tears really started to fall.

But I got four beers out of it, so sometimes life works out ok.

A Stroll Across Town

One good thing about Elk Grove, at least for me, is that everything is pretty much within walking distance of my shed. Granted, that "everything" doesn't constitute a whole lot, but then I don't exactly have a lot of money to spend anyway. Drugs are entertainment enough; who needs things like a movie theater, or even a place to rent a movie from? Do people even still do that?

So when I finally shuffled out of bed and got up and moving, it was only about a twenty-minute walk to the court house. The weather was nice enough, if a little on the hot side, but the tradeoff was about as pretty a sky as you could ever want. Bright enough to show you every little blight and scar the town had, but at the same time they didn't seem as bad in such a good light.

A pack of Pop-Tarts and a joint had been my breakfast. On the one hand, dealing with my aunt, I knew I wouldn't want to be all hopped up, as she had a way of getting under my skin. But I also wanted to be sharp. So a single joint was my compromise: calming without being too much so. It helped that what I had was really just skunkweed, so its effects were limited.

It was a little early for folks to be making their way to the square for lunch, so traffic was fairly sparse. Mostly old folks puttering around, headed to do whatever it was old people did. A few folks gave little waves in my direction, though I suspect poor eyesight had more to do with that than actual friendliness. The couple of people threading their way down the sidewalks near me were doing their level best to ignore their resident degenerate. To be fair, I didn't have any sort of strong desire to talk with them either.

The courthouse was far too stately a building for a place like Elk Grove, if you asked me, all fine red brick and white trim. Two stories tall with a bell tower atop it that reached up to the heavens in a way that polite folk likely found inspiring but to me was basically just a big middle finger. When I was younger, the bell had rung out every day at noon, but it had broke when I was just learning to drive and the city had never found the money to fix it. And I, for one, have always thought that to have a bit of poetry to it.

I crossed the street, a roundabout that encircled the courthouse like a moat, and took the stairs up to the front door two at a time. The city hadn't found the money to fix the bell, but they had, the year after 9/11, scraped up the funds to redo the entryway to keep us all safe from the terrorists. Because clearly Jubal County, Alabama, was a hotbed of jihadists.

What it meant was I had to pass through a metal detector watched over by Silas Warner. Silas, who had to be well into his late seventies, had the frail look of a man in his early nineties. Just what hardened terrorist he was supposed to stop was beyond me. More relevant, he had a serious hard-on toward yours truly for reasons I had never been able to fathom. I'm so fucking lovable.

I stepped in behind a young Black woman in a nice dress who Silas just waved around, not even bothering to drop her purse through the little x-ray machine. When he spotted me, however, his eyes narrowed.

"Court's tomorrow, Marsh, so you may as well go on now," he said. You could tell he was trying to muster up some real venom, but age had long ago defanged him, leaving his voice a thin whine.

"I ain't here for court," I offered with my winningest smile. The more chipper I was, the more it pissed him off. "Come to see my aunt."

How his eyes managed to narrow even more and still allowed him to see was a mystery for the ages. I was already emptying my pockets into the little plastic tray, though a few rolling papers, a set of keys, and a wallet didn't exactly take up a lot of space. I'd put the rolling papers in there on purpose just to rile the old fucker up, but he didn't seem to notice. He knew the game.

I stepped into the machine, and it beeped loudly.

"Belt, Marsh," the man said.

I removed my belt. I frequently went without one, but knowing I would run into Silas I made sure to put one on. With a smile, I stepped back in.

Beep.

"Check your pockets again," the man hissed.

Feeling around, I came up with a handful of change that I had purposefully forgotten, the last seventy-eight cents of my worldly riches. I put them in beside my wallet. I beamed at the old man, stepping back into the machine.

Beep.

Swearing, Silas staggered to his feet, scooping up the handheld detector and shuffling his way around to my side. Making him get up out of his seat was about the only victory I ever mustered in the courthouse. Usually I just ended up with a few days in jail or some fines. But hearing Silas curse under his breath—which came in old, wheezing bursts—well, it went just the tiniest way to evening the score.

Slowly he ran the detector over my front, which elicited no sound. At his command I obligingly swung around. As the wand passed over my ass, it beeped again. Dramatically, I slapped my forehead. "Oops!" I said, pulling out a pair of rusty nail clippers from my back pocket. "My bad, Silas."

The man didn't say anything worth repeating, just shuffled back to his seat and ran the little plastic box along the conveyor through the x-ray machine. Though what he expected to find inside an empty wallet, I have no idea. I guess at this point he was just trying to find something, anything on me to cause trouble. This wasn't my first rodeo, though.

Finally he handed my things back to me, frowning all the while. "Make it quick, Marsh. Don't waste working folks' time," he spat with all the invective and force of a spiteful three-year-old. I just gave a little wave and started making my way toward my aunt's office.

The courthouse on the outside could be confused for being stately. On the inside, it was just old and tired. White marble floors had gone dingy with age and decades of grubby feet, and the walls looked as though they had last been painted back when brown was considered an exciting color. The scattered benches had clearly seen more than their fair share of asses, and the only sign that looked more recent than the late seventies was one announcing that no guns were allowed. It was still kinda old, probably having gone up the same time as the metal detector, but it wasn't quite as faded as the rest.

My sneakers squeaked on the marble as I strode through the place. For all the good it did, they kept the floors slick and clean. Lipstick on a pig, if you asked me. But the long hallways that wrapped around the actual courtroom, my typical scene of battle, took me down to one last sign. It should have read "Abandon hope, all ye who enter here." Instead, it read "Probate Office."

Crystal's Method

Does the Marsh clan have a good reputation? No, not as such. For the most part it's fairly neutral, I guess you could say, most of the family just sorta blending in. A few are actively bad, I reckon, like my Daddy and, I suppose some might say, me. But most just get by like normal folks. Folks like HD and Krista.

Aunt Crystal definitely came down on the bad apple side of the family.

Slipping inside the office, I moved as quietly as possible. It wasn't actually possible to slip in unnoticed, but I was going for the element of surprise. Every little bit helped when dealing with Crystal.

A long, chest-high counter dominated the room. Behind it sat a trio of desks, but they were all empty. Instead the two women in the room were standing just behind the counter, each dealing with someone. The older of the two, a white woman in her fifties named Francis, frowned when she saw me. I had never seen the other lady, however, and she paid me little attention as she dealt with the old man in front of her who looked as though he was trying to file something.

I knew that to the right was the office of the probate judge, Willie Daniels. He was probably asleep, if I had to make a guess, or maybe eating. That was all he ever seemed to do, near as I could tell. He was a figurehead at best. The real power was to the left.

Moving quickly, I walked parallel to the counter and walked through an open doorway into a hallway so brown it could have been the inside of a tree. A closed door loomed there to my right, or at least that's how it seemed to me. A slightly more menacing brown than the rest of the hall, it was broken up by a small glass window with the words "Chief Probate Clerk" emblazoned on it in gold.

Fact of the matter was there was no such thing as a chief probate clerk in Jubal County. But Aunt Crystal had a way of getting what she wanted, and folks had long ago figured out it was best to just give in before things got nasty. So if putting some words on a door kept the dragon at bay, then words would go on the door.

I took a deep breath and bulled my way inside.

She was hunched there behind her desk, but as she looked up I saw not one iota of surprise or shock at someone just throwing her door wide. Her pinched face had a sour look about it, but then it always did. Her lips were pursed into a tight line, her dark eyes slightly narrowed.

"Howard Lee," she said, her voice sharp and grating. She was the only person who used my middle name, and the way she pronounced it made it sound like "cowardly." It pissed me right off, but then that's why she did it, so I tried my best to choke down a retort. Seeing as my surprise entry didn't seem to have her at all off-footed, I decided that maybe I should attempt charm. I was pretty sure I'd had some of that at some point.

"Aunt Crystal! Mighty fine seeing you today," I beamed.

She set her pen down and crossed her arms, saying nothing. She just sat there staring at me through her reading glasses, her face growing steadily more severe.

It was moments like this that had caused me to give her the private nickname of the Spider—not that I had ever been dumb enough to tell her, or anyone, about it. She huddled up in here, the center of a web of nastiness, waiting to pounce. She liked to see people squirm. And with her thin arms covered in thick black hairs, it always made me think of spider's legs.

There was a chair in front of her desk, but I was mighty hesitant to sit in it. I didn't want to be the fly in her web, squirming 'round nervous, but I was beginning to think that ship had sailed. I sorta took a half step to the chair, saw her jaw tighten, and froze.

I feared my Granny most in life, because she could lay a curse down the likes of which even God would fear. My daddy held second place in the Fear Olympics because I knew it was probably just a matter of time before he killed me. My Aunt Crystal, though? She ruined lives, and she didn't need magic or her fists to do it. And though I didn't have much of a life to speak of, I sure didn't want it ruined any more than it already was.

"Um, well . . ." I had to get it together. I thought of that drain in the floor, and the potential bad of that for a brief second eclipsed the potential bad of my aunt. "HD thought it would be a good idea for me to come speak at you for a bit."

Crystal snorted, that kind of snort you'd think only one of them old-school British noble types could pack that much disdain into. You'd be wrong, though. "Probably not, but we'll see."

I started to tell her the gist of what was going on. I left out some of the more magical details not because she wasn't a believer—she was—but because you always tried to get out of a conversation with Crystal while telling her as little as possible. If you gave her two and two, she like as not already had four, eight, twelve, and twenty from other sources, and she could whip it all together in some way to fuck you if you weren't real careful.

I started wrapping things up. "So, I'm just trying to see if you might know of anyone who might have it out for the old lady. Maybe an old flame, an affair gone wrong . . ."

She shook her head sharply. "That's the wrong tree you're barking up. I think I know who you're looking for, though. But telling you doesn't benefit me in any way I can see."

"I suppose pointing out how we're kin and all, bringing up family ties and such—that's also a wrong tree?" I asked.

She arched an eyebrow to such a severe point you could have stabbed someone with it. "If anything, it hurts your case."

I sighed. "What is it that you want?"

"Tell me about the night she died."

All of Granny's kids had some sort of power. HD somehow always knew when someone was coming over, about to call him, or was needing him. Rooster had his music. And of course my generation, the grandkids, a few of us had actual real magical ability, active style.

Crystal, though, no one knew what her power was exactly. Everyone was pretty sure it had something to do with finding out secrets, but she damn sure wasn't telling. She knew things she was never meant to know, should have had no way of knowing. And what she could do with them, hoarding them up and parceling them out years later like little sips of poison where they would do the most damage . . .

"No." It took everything in me to just say the word and not shout it.

Crystal didn't even bother to respond; she just went back to her paperwork. I was so mad, though, I was sorely tempted to slap the sheets right off that desk. Eyes seeing red, I was out the room and stomping into the hall before I realized it, the slamming of her door ringing in my ears.

Out of her presence I managed to calm down fractionally, enough that I was able to try and figure out why I had got as mad as I did. And when I tried it, I came to realize what my little, deep-down lizard brain knew before my upper monkey brain had been able to puzzle it together. It's not that she wanted to know about the worst day of my life.

It's that if she was asking, she thought there was more to the story than I knew.

I froze, and my mind sorta went blank for a second. It was like I did a reboot on my head, and it took a few seconds for it to turn back on. And when it did I was calm, cool, and collected—at least as much as a squirrelly little drug addict magician ever is. And I realized that she'd given me something, possibly without intending to. And that, coupled with hopefully getting somewhere with this damn curse, made opening her door and stepping back in worth it.

I'm not gonna lie, though, that smirk she had when I came back, it almost caused me to lose my cool. But I didn't.

And I got what I needed.

Shit Gets a Bit More—and Less—Real

It was nice of Krista to offer to come with me. And I knew that in all likelihood, nothing dramatic was going to happen and she would be just fine. But I also knew that if things went sideways, magic might start cropping up, and that was something she firmly wanted no part of. She knew it, too, which is the only reason why she let me go it alone, I think. Seeing that lingering guilt on her face was both delicious in that I knew next fight I would have some fresh ammunition, and painful because at the end of the day she really was my best friend.

So I had her drop me off at the end of the dirt road the Durrant family mostly all lived on. It was a good mile down the road to where I was going, but I wanted that time to get my head on straight and to find a little dark corner to do a little drugs. The harder stuff that Krista tried putting her head in the sand about.

I didn't expect much of a fuss, but if I found a good excuse to take a shitload of drugs and file it under "preparedness," I was gonna use it. I also wanted a little meth to wash the taste of having to deal with Aunt Crystal out my mouth. I felt like I was walking around with tiny little strands of her web still clinging to me, making me feel foul and dirty. But it got me what I wanted. Least I was 99.9% sure, that is.

I couldn't really remember who'd said it now, but someone had mentioned Delva Durrant and had said she got a little slice of land cut off for her when her father died. That the old lady Jane had kindly gave her a bit to make a life on. And turns out that while that was true, Crystal had the rest of the story.

You see, Delva had been written out her daddy's will for being with a Black man. The old goat clearly wasn't the most tolerant of folks, and with no other heirs it all went to Jane. Every damn acre—of which it appeared was quite a large number of them—was chock-full of cows and trees and all sorts of other valuable goodies.

I don't know how true it was, but Crystal even said the reason Delva wasn't at the funeral wasn't because she was off shacked up but because on his deathbed, her daddy had forbidden anyone to let her know about his funeral.

That he didn't want her there, that she was no daughter of his.

If that kinda shit don't make you bitter, I'm not sure what will.

Delva didn't have the kind of money to contest the will, and in that day and age I doubt it would have done any good if she had. Hell, in *this* day I don't know that it would. I'm no legal expert—unless you count time spent getting ground up in the gears of justice as legal experience—so what the fuck do I know, really?

Regardless, she didn't have any sort of legal recourse, so she proceeded to make her family's life as much of a living hell as possible. All sorts of mischief ranging from stealing mail to running over a dog by "mistake." She may have even burned down a barn, though no one was ever able to prove it. Whatever Delva may have been, she was sure as hell vindictive and clever.

Finally, Jane had enough, and that's when she broke off a little chunk for her sister. Only it was the most worthless acres in the whole lot, being what amounted to a big ol' stretch of red clay where even the grass had a hard time growing. It was enough to quiet Delva down to the point that she stopped actively trying to ruin folks' lives, though.

At least that's what everyone would have thought, only looking at everything, it's pretty clear she didn't give up.

She went to Morgan and got her to whip up a curse that would kill her sister and all her grand young'uns. I reckon she figured that she might not live to inherit everything. I mean, there were Jane's kids in the picture, but eventually everything would revert to her side of the family. She was playing the long, spiteful game, and hurting her sister was just as important as winning.

It wasn't fucking *Hamlet*, but then Jubal County damn sure ain't Denmark.

It was trying to get on fairly late in the day. It wouldn't be fair to say the sun was setting, really, but it looked of a mind to really start the process up here soon. So it was bright out, but there was a hint of dim to it all. Like that sun was getting anxious and wanted to go hide behind the treetops off to my right.

It was pastures off in that direction, all open green spaces up until they went crashing up against a pine thicket maybe a quarter mile away. I didn't see any cows, but you could see piles of dried shit dotting the landscape between the low mounds of fire ant beds. To my left, though, the trees were right up against the road, and taking a quick glance around to make sure no one was eyeing me, I slipped into the shadowy undergrowth to hunch down behind a tree.

I may have hovered my way back to the road a few minutes later, maybe flown a bit, even. Of course I can't fly—that shit's impossible, I think—but it damn sure felt like it. I was feeling like a million bucks. Tomorrow, I would feel like someone had lit that pile of money on fire and stomped it out, but for the moment I was shit hot. Perhaps a bit twitchy, but shit hot.

Warm sun on my face, a cocktail of drugs coursing through my veins, a gentle breeze that felt like a billion tiny fairy fingers softly caressing my skin with feather dusters . . .

I walked. *Power* walked. Walked with AUTHORITY. I was a force to be reckoned with, and by God—no, by GAWD! The world had better recognize. The inner debate was a war of egos as to whether I should be running or not. Being fast as a cheetah in a blender, I would look mighty impressive sprinting down the road. But a part of me wondered if that was a stately enough look for someone as regal as myself. And would the cutoff fringe hanging down from my jorts tickle my knees? It would all be ruined if I was cackling from tickled knees. I could pull the knife from my pocket and cut the fringe, but then I liked the fringe. It added a bit of panache anytime I wasn't running. I wondered when the last time I had actually run was. Maybe when the King came after me? I wonder what the big fucking catfish was up to, whatever his name was. I mean, I knew it, but I decided I couldn't remember it to keep myself safe. If I couldn't remember his name, he couldn't remember mine, and then he couldn't come calling for a favor. He couldn't find me. I bet his whiskers would tickle like my jean fringe. I bet that's why he kept in the water, rather than going around running on land. That and not having legs, that is. Running on fins would look even sillier than running with tickled knees. I wondered when the last time I'd had catfish was. Preach's had good fried catfish but I didn't go there all that often, things being what they were. That BBQ smell, though—I could damn near smell it! I mean, I couldn't with the smell of dusty road and old cow shit and grass and something that would probably have me sneezing sometime next week and . . . well, I guess it was getting on time for me to take a bath. Maybe Krista would let me take a shower at her place. It was bullshit that Krista wouldn't show me how to do any good magic. I damn sure didn't like being a part of shit like this, but did you see me throwing hissy fits all the time? No, I just got shit done without bitching. As was befitting of someone as got-damn magnificent as me.

I was walking the wrong way.

Of course when I realized this, my one tiny moment of fallibility, my one split second of a minor, teensy little mistake, the kind anyone could make, then there was a cow watching me. Did I detect a bit of judgment in its brown eyes?

You're goddamn right I did.

It was that damn Brahman bull, all grays and darker smudges with a tall hump on its back. Its ears drooped, its neck skin was damn near like a turkey waddle, and its jaw was just steadily making cud. It was the most handsome bull in the world, I had no doubt. But it had seen my foible and was trying to sit in judgment of me, a far superior being, no matter how handsome a bull he was.

A few muttered words and an outflinging of my hands later, a sound like thunder roared out, startling the Brahman. It was so scared it shit as it ran, disappearing over a low rise in a rumble of hoof beats. It was just noise, but it was enough to wipe that smug look off that damn cow's face.

It also managed to knock just enough off my high to make me realize that maybe I had been a bit too high. Perhaps even a *lot* too high. In retrospect, I decided that I had overdone it a bit back behind that tree, and with a little wiggle of my fingers I burned off a bit more. Just to even myself out. I mean, I had to be able to talk to folks, and the kind of guy who thinks a cow is judging him is perhaps not the best person for that job.

Time wasn't limitless, so I set off at a brisk walk, this time in the right direction. I didn't run; I wasn't as high anymore, and I would have to be either a lot more drunk, or a lot more scared, to set these wheezing smoker's lungs to a task like that.

The trees thinned then all but disappeared as I got closer to Delva's. I could see the place clearly and was just as impressed by it with a longer look as I had been with my fleeting glances from the car rides, which is to say not at all. It was a little rise of red clay, without even one good tree for shade.

Two trailers, one so ratty I would choose my shed over it any day, were hunched there on top. They sat crossways to one another, each at an angle to the road, making a shallow V. Within the sweeping, rusty arms of that embrace were a few cars, most of which likely hadn't run in many a year, and the usual assortment of trash, cast-off toys, and scraggly weeds. Grass couldn't hack it there, but some weeds are hardier stuff.

Still squatted on her ratty plastic folding chair throne was a doughy, wrinkled woman basking in the shade of a beach umbrella. I had a suspicion that the trailers very likely had no AC, maybe not even power at the moment, and so the family matriarch had settled outside where it would be a bit less stuffy.

The yard was empty save for her, though there were several other chairs dotting the area around her. The red clay was practically white with cigarette butts and ash, no doubt the fallen siblings of the Virginia Slim drooping from one corner of Delva's mouth. At least an inch of ash threatened to fall at any moment, but the old woman was too busy shelling peas to bother flicking it off.

She eyed me as I stepped into the yard, watery brown eyes drifting toward me before turning back to the bucket of peas in her lap. The peas plinked into a metal container at her feet—*tink, tink, tink, tink*—a steady, metallic rainfall of produce. She did something with her mouth which sent the ash falling, but away from her so it didn't fall on her shirt.

"Evenin'," she said from around her cigarette. Her voice was gravelly, and her tone let it be known she was stating a fact, not trying to be inviting.

I decided to cut to the heart of things while there was no one around to complicate matters. "You Delva?"

"Who wants to know?"

"Name's Howard Marsh," I offered.

She looked over at me again, her eyes a little harder now. "I reckon you would be. You look like a lot like your Granddaddy."

"So they tell me. Don't rightly remember, myself." My memories from those years have an awful lot of blank spaces, which stung. I'd no idea this woman had known my family, though I suppose it made sense.

"Why're you here, Howard Marsh? Come to buy a mess of peas?"

I reached into my pocket and pulled a pack of cigs, then went fishing for a lighter to pair with them. "I reckon you know why a Marsh would be here."

She sat the bucket down and pulled out her lighter, tossing it to me. I caught it, which half surprised me. "Yeah," she said with a sigh, "I reckon I do."

Taking that first blessed drag on my smoke, I stepped over and handed back her lighter. It was solid white and, had I noticed before then, I might would have let it drop. "All white lighters are bad luck, you know," I said as she took it.

She burst into bitter laughter, a grating, chalky sound like brittle rocks crunching underfoot. She waved a hand around behind her. "Damn, wouldn't that be terrible, to have a run of bad luck all of a sudden? Just when things was going so damn good."

I snorted, shaking my head a bit. "That it would."

"Your Granny send you?" she asked, her face growing serious once again.

I debated how to answer that, using a pull on my smoke to buy me time. It would probably be to my advantage to say she had, but then it wasn't that wise to make claims about Granny that weren't true. She had a way of hearing things you wouldn't think she could. "Not directly," I said by way of internal compromise, letting the words hang there a moment. "One way or another, your sister'll be dead soon. Don't need no curse to finish the job at this point. Tell me where you tucked it, and I'll do the rest."

She didn't say anything for a time, just sitting hunched there. Cutting a little sigh, she turned and looked at me. "You know, thought I could hold this hate forever. It was hawt at one point, 'bout fit to burn me up."

I knew how that felt. "What happened?"

"Life. When you only got so much time and energy, sometimes you just ain't got it to spare on hate when you just trying to keep your head above water. I still hate 'em, and they was damn sure wrong for what they done. But . . . well . . . fuck it." She spat. "Not like any of mine would do anything but let the land turn to ruin—that or sell it off to buy pills. And what's the damn point then? Fuck it."

She hobbled to her feet, shuffling to one side, and pointed off behind the trailers. Back a ways was a tree line, mostly pine but with a few oaks and the like there to spice things up. "The family plot is back in there. The old one, where Daddy and Momma are buried. Jane's got a plot back there all laid out; Daddy bought it for her. Look for a handful of white rocks. Under that, about a foot down, you'll find the jar. Morgan said breaking that jar would stop things."

"You hid it in her own grave?" I grimaced. "That's some cold, poetic shit right there."

"A fuckin' poet, that's me," she grinned sardonically. "Now get on with ya. I got work to do."

I nodded and set off in the direction she pointed out. I had to thread my way through various mounds of trash, some of which I bet had to be decades old, if not longer. I was half afraid of getting snakebit, having to walk around such. But soon enough I reached the rusty two-strand barbed wire fence and passed through easily enough. The farther I walked, the more the ground came to life. It really did look like Jane had set her sister on the only dead spot in the whole area.

It made me wonder, though, how much of it was natural and how much was an echo from that curse. You don't work big hoodoo like that without at least a little blowback, I find. Had bad earth been turned even more barren by that old lady's hate? No way to tell, but it left me thinking, that's for sure.

I could see the clearing of the family plot before I even entered the trees. It wasn't far back at all, which made me think that as old as the plot looked to be, the trees around it were all likely younger than the graveyard. The woods behind it certainly seemed a bit darker looking, least from where I stood.

There were a dozen stones holed up within a low wrought iron fence. It was damn near full up with headstones, which I supposed was why the place wasn't getting any more use at this point. I supposed Jane would be the last to find her way here. Another generation and I bet this whole place would just be swallowed up by the woods, and you'd have to trip over it to find it.

The gate was rusted shut, but the fence was low enough I was able to just step over it. A bit of my jort fringe got caught, but it was easy enough to pull free and I was able to escape without any serious injury to flesh or jeans. It was a true Christmas miracle.

It wasn't hard to find Jane's plot; it was the most recent stone of them all. It had been white once, I was pretty sure, but time and lichen had turned it more of a grayish black, though the letters were all still legible. That was saying more than most of the headstones.

The weeds were pretty well grown up, but with a little looking and shuffling with my boots I was able to find the rocks. They looked like someone had painted a handful of gravel, but they stood out well enough. Using my heel I was able to kick back the rocks and scrape away the top layer of grass and weeds. The dirt beneath it was surprisingly dark and loamy; I fully expected to hit clay.

Crouching down, I began to scoop handfuls of dirt, slinging them wide. I didn't much care if anyone knew what I did. I figured if anyone saw this hole, they would assume it was an armadillo what had done it. So I dug away, happy as a very high clam, until my hands hit something hard and smooth.

With a shout of triumph, I pulled out an old mason jar, its lid just about rusted solid. Inside I could see all manner of shit: a few bones, some very dead greenery, some sort of liquid. The usual hodgepodge of a spell jar. I looked hard at it, then hurled the jar into Mrs. Jane's headstone. It shattered with a most pleasing sound.

Then shit got a little more real than I would have liked.

You Done Fucked Up Now

I didn't realize it at first. The jar shattered, and I figured that would be that. Which was really dumb of me, in retrospect. If breaking the jar was all it took to break the curse, then you wouldn't have to be "good" at curse breaking like Granny was. But I was high. And high Marsh isn't really thinking Marsh.

I was half turned away to start heading back when a roiling bit of gray caught the corner of my vision. Smoke came billowing out of the shattered glass shards of the jar. Like an idiot I breathed in a bunch of putrid egg-smelling air, which made me choke. I was coughing up a storm in a heartbeat, trying not to throw up from how bad it smelled. It burned as I breathed it in, stinging my nostrils and leaving me sorta gasping.

Through watery eyes I saw a swarm of flies come churning up from those shattered ruins. They were fat, bloated blue-black flies that whipped up a noxious sort of buzzing. The droning noise filled my ears, not the least of which was because that swarm washed across my face trying to fill every hole.

I could feel their tiny hairs and wings slapping at my face, and I waved my arms trying to knock them away. I felt them crunch between my teeth as I shouted, and I choked and spat trying to get them out. I could feel them wiggling in my ears and nose. It might have tickled if it hadn't been so terrifying and disgusting.

My feet stepped in to take over as my brain was locked down in disgust and I took to running. I was half blind, but I could see well enough to not run into any trees, I was pretty sure. Thick weeds tugged at my feet, but I was pounding away pretty damn quick.

I didn't see the low metal fence that surrounded the graveyard, and in my panic I had forgotten all about it. Metal struck flesh and I went hurtling head over heels. I screamed in pain, not totally sure I hadn't just broken my shins. My rapid descent had shook the flies loose, though, at least for a moment—long enough that I could see the blood welling up from gashes in my legs.

Managing to stagger to my feet, I found my legs weren't broken, though they just near about felt that way. Blood was flowing pretty freely down from just below my knees, and I could see flecks of rust mixed in with the red. I wondered how lockjaw was going to feel, because the way my luck went, that seemed inevitable.

The flies seemed to have moved on, but the smoke was still boiling up from the ground. It was caught in the light breeze and was spreading out, making a layer about like fog. It filled the space between the fence, growing steadily thicker. It stopped at the fence line for no reason I could see, but then that's magic for you. The smoke was contained, and the flies were gone, so I figured all was well. Just the aftereffects of a curse breaking.

Then I saw the eyes.

In the heart of the smoke, glowing yellow eyes peered out at me. They winked in and out, like static almost, but the glow lingered in the moments the eyes were gone, making them seem more constant than they were. They eased forward through the thick clouds, and as they neared I could see the outline of a snout begin to form.

The Flicker Dog had arrived, and he looked pissed. The closer it got, the more it seemed to solidify. It still flashed away for split seconds, but the flashes grew more frequent and more spaced apart, which made it all the more easy to see the mighty big teeth the fucker had. The damn thing was drooling up a storm, no doubt hungry for a taste of Marsh. I didn't aim to let it get one, however.

I turned and ran. I wasn't sure if it could make it outside that fog or if it would even last longer than a couple more seconds. I mean, I didn't know shit, and the sudden realization that I took my advice on how to break this curse from a woman with absolutely no magical ability caused my butthole to tighten so hard I could have ate coal and shit a diamond.

A glance back over my shoulder had three effects. First, it showed that damn dog flickering right through the fence, coming out the other side as though it hadn't even been there. This in turn caused me to keep looking a bit longer than I should have, which finally led to me tripping over some sort of stick. I hit my legs again, pine needles jabbing into my leg wounds and causing me to howl in pain.

My howl was echoed by the Flicker Dog. It sounded as though it was coming from a far distance, reaching my ears from miles away and not just thirty feet or so. It was a haunting sound that sent a chill down my spine, thick with sadness and lingering anger. It burrowed its way down into my soul, and all thought went running.

My reality became tiny snippets that were a jumbled mess. They may have come out of order, but who was I to say? A limb clawed my face, leaving a long scratch across my cheek running from my chin to the corner of my eye. A glimpse of the setting sun trying to melt down behind distant trees. The flickering glance of glowing eyes coming from my left, then my right, seconds apart maybe. Another trip, caught on hands that were oddly bloody.

The scattered moments managed to solidify into one coherent sliver when I ran into Delva's yard. She was standing there on a sagging porch cackling with laughter. I was far too fear addled to come up with some sort of pithy retort, instead focusing all my energy on running as fast as my aching legs and burning lungs would allow.

"Run, Marsh, run!" she brayed. "Get fucked, boy! Enjoy messing in things that don't fuckin' concern ya!"

My smoker's lungs were not having it. But the terror was so thick on me that I couldn't stop running. I felt like I was being compelled or something, like the fear wasn't exactly natural. It was only as the barbed wire fence of the pasture across from Delva's raked across my back that I realized that was probably exactly what was going on.

Still running, I managed to work my fingers and gasp out a few words and I felt the terror fade away. The fear was still there, but it felt normal, right. It wasn't full of the mindlessness that had been hounding me. I slowed to a jog, looking around for the Flicker Dog.

It was a dozen feet away to my right, tongue lolling as its eyes gazed at me hungrily. It was easily keeping pace with me, so I stopped and turned to face it head-on. It slowed and after a few steps it, too, came to a stop.

Calling on my power, my hand ignited into flame. "Bad dog," I muttered as I hurled the fire at its stupid fucking face.

I swear the damn thing laughed at me as it flickered. Just as my flame should have hit, it vanished, reappearing a split second later. The fire struck the pasture, catching a small patch of grass alight, brightening the gloaming a bit.

The dog raised its head, sniffing deeply, then took off at a run. It bolted faster than any dog had the right to be, steadily just a-flickering away. It was headed away from me, though, so I was ok with it. To be honest, if it was just going to flicker out every time I tried to hit it with a spell, I was pretty much fucked. So being as far away from the damn thing seemed my best ploy at the moment. I could maybe get up with HD and we could figure this part out before it killed me.

It occurred to me then that it had headed north. As in the direction of Montgomery. Had it taken off to go kill Hank? To finish the job it had started? That made sense, kinda, but then it also made no sense. I suspected that old bitch Delva had tricked me into making myself into the object of the curse, which was why the dog had started after me. So why would it suddenly run off like that? It set me on edge about as bad as when the critter had first lit out after me.

I walked over to the burning patch of grass and set out to stomping it out. You had to be careful with magical fire like this; it had a tendency to cling a bit better than normal flames. I wasn't on the best of terms with the Durrant family, and I figured if I burned up their pasture land, that wouldn't exactly help mend any fences. It took a good minute or so, and I melted the soles of my boots a little, but I got it out.

That's when I heard the rumble.

Where's the Beef?

It wasn't dark yet, not really, but it was working at it real hard. It was dark enough though that it took a few moments for me to figure out just what was causing all that ruckus. Then I saw it come into view, rightly into view, and I cursed up a blue streak.

It was that Brahman bull. The grayness of its hide meshed in well with the creeping darkness, and honestly it was more the movement that caught my eye initially. It was coming at me at a pretty good clip, its hooves making that thundering noise I heard. Damn thing had to weigh at least a ton, easily, and its horns were lowered and looking to handle some business from the looks of things.

I'd have thought maybe it was just coming back to avenge the indignity I had put it through earlier if I hadn't seen its eyes flickering with golden light.

All the slots kindly clicked into place. This damn Flicker Dog was scaring folks into positions that it could use the world around it to finish them off. My guess was it couldn't directly act on our world; it was too much a part of the other. It was an interesting thought, and in that moment far, far less important than getting the fuck out of the way of a ton of trampling hamburger with an attitude.

I was too far from the fence, and I had a guess the damn thing would just ignore the barbed wire. Not like it was in control of its own body, and what the hell would a spirit dog care about the damage done to a body it was possessing? So that wouldn't do me any good.

Ignoring my still not-yet-recovered lungs, I ran. There was a stunted little cedar close enough that I stood at least a little chance of reaching it before catching them hooves. I knew I would need to fight it, but I wasn't thinking real clearly still, and I wanted at least a second to get my bearings. If it came down to it, I'd fight before we reached the tree, but I damn sure didn't want to have to.

You ever have your brain just lock in on something stupid in the midst of something important? Every step I ran—every aching, burning, curse filled step—all I could think of was if I knocked it over, I could call it "ground beef." It was so stupid, but it's all I could think about. Maybe it helped, because I kinda hated myself more at that moment than I was scared of the Flicker Dog. Or maybe my brain had decided it wanted to punish me one last time before I died.

I didn't even take the second it would have taken to glance back. Those hooves sounded so fucking close, but the tree was suddenly right there in front of me. I didn't slow as I hit it, using my momentum to try to and just run up the side of it.

But I am not Bruce Lee.

A few steps up the side, my feet of course slid right the fuck down. Gravity was doing what it does best, and I had a one way ticket to stomped death. But stretching my arms out, I was able to grab hold of the lowest limb.

The bark of it tore at my palms but I held on, my eyes scrunching up in pain. My feet dangling, my body weight trying to pull me down, I managed to tug myself up, getting my gut up over the limb. I was trying to pull a leg up and over when the bull arrived.

It slammed into that tree with all the momentum that two thousand plus pounds of stampeding cow could muster. It was fast coming to me that the laws of physics were not my friends today. The tree rocked so hard I almost fell right back down. I had to scramble to keep up in my tiny sanctuary and the bark was roughing up my skin something fierce. Worst of all, the tree had taken on a bit of a lean to it.

With a grunt, I managed to get up in the tree proper. I was holding on to one of the higher up branches, my feet planted as firmly as I could manage to the one I had initially used to struggle up. The bull was standing there below me, looking up at me with glowing eyes, just a-huffing.

It came to me that if that dog couldn't touch me in its spirit form, then I probably couldn't touch it back. But if it could use the bull to touch me, then . . .

Before I could follow that thought much further, the damn thing slammed into the tree again. It didn't have all the momentum this time, but a ton is a ton no matter how you slice it. It smacked the tree and the whole thing rocked a little farther to the side. That first blow had loosened up its roots pretty solidly, it seemed, and it was now kicked out at a pretty damn noticeable lean. It wouldn't take too many more of those to knock the tree right—

It hit again. I about fell out this time, the tree knocked wide enough that I wasn't standing up straight so much as clinging on for my life so as I didn't fall back down toward the trunk. Which would put me in slamming range, I reckoned. It was do or die time—literally.

"Hey!" I yelled out. Sure enough the bull stopped, looking up at me.

I leapt.

I can't do a whole lot of different things with my magic, but I can feed it into my muscles kinda, making me stronger. Not strong enough to stop a charging bull—not without a lot more preparation, at least—but strong enough to hold on.

My hands found its horns as I fell on its damn head. They grabbed on, my body falling across its stupid face, its hard skull partially winding me. I didn't care; I just grabbed onto those horns and pulled down as hard as I could.

The bull's head lowered gradually while it snorted and raged. It was trying to sling me around, but my arms were holding its head still enough that it couldn't get up the momentum. It was pulling me side to side sure, but I didn't need to hold on too long.

From the magic I was feeding into my arms, I sent a thread of the same power that summoned up that fire I sling around. The horns began to smoke and glow, which smelled damn awful. The bull smelled it, too, and even though the pain hadn't hit yet, it wasn't having it.

With a bellow it pushed forward. My feet dug into the ground, but that just slowed it. Within a few moments it had me pushed back against the tree. Granted, it gave me something more substantial to push back from, but my magic was far from limitless. If I was lucky, I might have a minute of magic left in me the way I was burning it, and then I would be turned into potted meat.

I pushed as much magic into my limbs as I could handle, maybe even a touch more than I should have, but it was go time, goddamn it. It cut the time I had left in half, probably, but with a life like mine cutting it shorter was probably just doing me a bit of a favor, honestly. Still, I had to risk it for the biscuit.

The heat was spreading through its skull. I could see smoke starting to rise from its hide. Ever put a flashlight in your mouth in the dark and looked in a mirror? That reddish glow under your skin—ever seen that? That's what it looked like. It was beginning to smell like the world's worst barbecue as its gray hide began to crackle and char.

The heat and stench washed over me, and it started to get too hot for me to stand. I ain't really all that fireproof. When the sweat in my clothes began to steam I sent a last push, every last stitch of magic I had, down my arms in one last burst.

It staggered me, and I jumped to one side as best I could. I fell to the ground, weak as a kitten, but I frantically started trying to get up and get away, sure I was gonna get stomped any second. But instead of the sound of a hoof crunching my skull, I just heard bellows and the sound of a skull smacking the tree.

Getting a few feet away, I risked a look back. That bull was all caught up in flame, and it had spread to the tree. Old and withered as it was, that tree went up like a torch made of a lightered stump. The bull, being made of delicious meats, did much the same.

The tree catching and burning there against the evening sky was as beautiful as that bull writhing and dying was terrible. It turned my stomach, to be honest, and I was pretty sure it was gonna be some time before I could eat beef again. I had to watch, though, and make sure that damn dog didn't go running out.

It wasn't my first rodeo with keeping a spirit trapped up in a skull, and I didn't aim to take any chances. So I stood there and watched as my magical fire burned that bull away till all that was left was a charred black skull. And once it had cooled, I snagged it up and started walking back to the road, to Krista.

Welcome to My Life

K rista stood there looking kinda awkward. She had on a black dress, real prim and proper, which was about as out of place in my shed home as you could get. Her gaze kept drifting to my back wall, where a certain blackened skull had taken up a position beside my black-and-yellow painted deer skull. She wasn't asking any questions, though.

"It was a nice service. Mrs. Jane was a well-loved lady," she was saying. "And seeing Hank there, well, that was nice."

It was now a month or so after all the bullshit had gone down. The curse was broke, Jane died all natural like, and Hank was all good. Rutherford had even not threatened to have me killed, which I figure was probably as close to an "attaboy" as I would ever get from him.

"His parents, they asked after you. I think they wanted you there."

I rolled my eyes. "No, they didn't. They ain't even thanked me, you know?"

"I know," she said, looking down at her feet.

She stayed quiet for a few moments, and with me being focused on rolling up a fat joint, I didn't exactly carry the conversation. So it was right silent for a few moments, then she started back.

"I, uh . . . I kinda get it now."

I looked over at her. "Get what?"

"You," she said. "Why you're like you are. At least a little. You do these things, hard things, with no thanks or anything. You can't even really tell folks what you do, because who would believe you? And you got nothing to really go by. No training, I mean." She looked guilty as she said it. I let her speak, wanting to see where this was going.

"You're kinda carrying my load for me. Or what was supposed to be my load, if I hadn't turned my back on that life. And you got nothing to show for it all but a lot of grief. You saved a boy's life, and no one even thanked you. That's bullshit, Howard."

I snorted. "Welcome to my life. One endless string of bullshit."

"Yeah," she said softly, then she straightened. "So look, I am not the person to take that load from you. But maybe I can make it a little easier to carry. I thought . . . I thought I might show you something Granny taught me that might help you out. You know her crow, Magda? Her familiar? I can teach you how to make your own. I don't know how well I remember a lot of what she taught me—and probably not well enough to teach you, at least—but that I can do."

I was stunned. She had tried to never even acknowledge she'd learned anything like that, and here she was now willing to teach me.

"Please," was all I could manage to say. It came out as a whisper, and I hoped it didn't sound too desperate.

A World of Possibilities

It was evening. I'd been sitting there all afternoon waiting for some sort of bird to come close enough to put what Krista had showed me into practice. And by some bird, I meant a *cool* bird. Not some shit-ass sparrow or something. In a pinch, I would take a blue jay or cardinal. But I wanted something badass like a crow or owl. I might would even settle for a buzzard! That would be kinda cool.

Being patient wasn't my strong suit, but for this I had managed. And it had paid off. Not fifty yards away on the powerline was a fucking hawk. I hadn't even considered how badass that would be. So I started voicing the words, getting my mind right, sending the magic flowing out of me into the glyph I'd chalked onto the ground. I closed my eyes and opened myself up, just a-praying I was doing this right.

Then I felt a pulse spark out from that sigil, and I knew it had happened. I'd done it. I called out with my mind, telling my new buddy to come to me. I opened my eyes and looked to that hawk.

It just sat there.

I could feel the connection—it was there. Why the fuck was it ignoring me?! I could have sworn I could feel it coming closer, even though this jumble of feelings was all sorts of new to me. But still, that hawk just chilled there.

A rustle came to my ears then. It was coming from the dumpster over behind the Dairy Queen, and as I looked I saw the fattest possum I had ever seen in my life come waddling out through the fence. It was grinning up a storm, its fur slick with grease and melted ice cream, no doubt.

It tottered over right to my feet, looking up at me with its ugly little face.

"Fuck it," I laughed, scooping the heavy sumbitch up.

The Back Matter!

About the Author

Born and raised in South Alabama, Bob is an author, podcaster, tabletop game designer, and all around hot mess. His cause of death will most likely result from one of the hitchhikers with he picks up reckless abandon. A study in contrasts, he once skinny-dipped at a wedding and is also an Eagle Scout. He has two useless college degrees, has roadied for bands, and broke his wrist in a wall of death at a Divine Heresy show. He's written for video games, designed board games, and owns a disturbing number of roleplaying games. When he was eight he give a camel a coke in Israel and got flashed in Paris. When he grew up he watched a monkey steal a man's wallet in Costa Rica. He's made passible podcasts, filmed terrible short horror movies, and been the producer on a trio of albums you've never heard of. Thriving on the groans of those he has punned around he spends far too much time nervously laughing. He once dug up a dead cow in a creek thinking it was a human cadaver and has a cousin that's a water witch. In college he gave haunted ghost tours (even though he's pretty sure ghosts aren't real). He's been stalked, gave a Prophet a lift, and been stagger drunk in more states than he would care to admit.

Growing up, he was always jealous of the wide variety of jobs his favorite authors listed in their 'about the author' sections, not fully realizing what a hellscape he was lusting after. So to that end Bob has been in no particular order: a warehouse clerk, a roadie for a band, pizza delivery guy, grocery store bag boy, telephone survey giver, inventory manager, quit Walmart after only three days, and currently works in IT. Learn from him sweet children, and flee now to the woods and leave behind the world of men.

More relevant he wrote this book, some other books, and has been published by a number of other folks with questionable judgement. The fictional things he writes sometimes come weirdly true. He lives in the middle of Alabama with his amazing LadyWife, the Kiddo, and a number of increasingly portly cats.

You can learn more at **www.talesbybob.com**

Reviews!

Did you leave a review? In the immortal words of Mathew McConaughey: "It'd be a lot cooler if you did."

Email List!

If you want to keep up with news about my books, this is the best way! I'll never sell or share my email list, and I promise to never bother you more than once a month (unless, like, its super-mega-secret important). To sign up go to my website: **www.talesbybob.com**

Patreon!

If you want even more Bob content, then go check out his Patreon. It's full of short stories, flash fictions, even draft copies of books. Big news also gets announced there before anywhere else, along with sneak peaks of book covers and other behind the scenes content. A popular series on there are 'The Marsh Dispatches' which is an ongoing series of essays written from the perspective of Howard Marsh the Methgician. Check out **www.patreo n.com/talesbybob**

Transparency!

When I started out, I had no other authors that I knew well enough to ask questions about sales numbers, social media growth, etc. I had no idea if my sales numbers were good, bad, or somewhere in-between. But seeing as I'm a big believer in the concept of *'be the change you want to see'* I started sharing all that information in hopes that it would motivate other authors to do the same. And even if they don't, at least this information is available to anyone who wants to know what those types of stats look like for a small time author like myself. So if you visit my website you can see all sorts of behind the scenes information each month, like how my social media grew (or shrank), how sales were, what I tried differently that month, etc. I also break down my stats around my book launches and get into the nitty gritty of each major in person event I do. Check out **www.talesbybob.com/transparency-project**

Education!

I have been helped by countless other creatives and authors along my journey. So anything I can do to pay that help forward, I do. That's why as much as possible I try to keep a host of free resources on my website folks to learn from. If I get paid to teach a workshop, I usually turn it into a youtube video and share the powerpoint I used along with it. If I get asked the same question enough times I will turn it into a blog post or video. I also offer up 'intern' opportunities for folks who want to learn in person sales. And if you want something more in depth, check out my book "Create Your Way to Freedom! How

To Be A Big Success From Someone Who Isn't!" Check out **www.talesbybob.com/education**

Podcasts!

Bob does a lot podcasting. You should go to his website, **www.talesbybob.com** (noticing a theme here?), and check them out. Most of them are related to books in some way, but not all! His best known historically has been Books, Beards, Booze.

Book Clubs!

Want to read this book as part of your book club? Reach out! If you are close enough, I might come speak to it (especially if yall have good snacks). If you are farther away, I might be available to speak to your group remotely. At the bare minimum I will shoot you an email with some bonus content of some sort, and some book club discussion questions. Just us the contact form on my website, **www.talesbybob.com/contact**

About Bearded Bard Inkworks

A real human book publisher, who puts out novels and ttrpgs!

Here at Bearded Bard Inkworks, we are human people, who put out books, and things like books. Booky things. With actual pages. And ink. Except when they're digital of course. Either way, we're absolutely people, and not at all three octopuses pretending to be book publishers. Just look at the top hats. Only a human could be so fashionable.

Look, we love books here at Bearded Bard Inkworks. We do. But we also love rpgs. And general weirdness. So we seek out authors who are exploring unique spaces, while also generating cool tabletop games. Because who doesn't love the idea of finding that next book they love, and then getting to play a game in that world?

Learn more at **www.beardedbardinkworks.com**

STRUGGLING WITH DRUG ADDICTION?

If you or someone you know is struggling with drug addiction and want to get help, then call the number below. It is the Substance Abuse and Mental Health Services Administration help line, a confidential, free, 24-hour-a-day, 365-day-a-year, information service, in English and Spanish, for individuals and family members facing mental and/or substance use disorders. This service provides referrals to local treatment facilities, support groups, and community-based organizations. Callers can also order free publications and other information.

1-800-662-HELP (4357)

For more information you can visit their website here:

www.samhsa.gov/